Peace and Love

Huskyteer

Peace and Love

Production copyright FurPlanet Productions © 2023

Cover Artwork © Idess Artist 2023
Peace symbol by Vecteezy.com

Published by FurPlanet Productions
Dallas, Texas
www.FurPlanet.com

eBook ISBN 978-1-61450-604-1
Paperback ISBN 978-1-61450-603-4

First Edition Trade Paperback 2023

This is a work of fiction. All characters and events portrayed within are fictitious.

Contents

For my dad, a groovy cat.

Peace Man

Roger felt the cloud of irritation start to build around him as he walked from his car to the front door, sidestepping the elderly otter woman in the weird clothes who always tried to engage him in conversation and noting that the 'FOXES AGAINST THE WAR' banner he'd made his roomie take down from the living-room window was back in position. Turning the key in the lock, he sent up a silent litany:

Please let Frank have the rent money ready.

Please don't let Frank be burning incense again.

Please don't say Frank's invited his hippie friends over.

The smell of smoky jasmine hit him as soon as he walked into the hall. Female laughter came from the front room, along with the sound of a guitar strumming one chord over and over again. Roger sighed, rolled his eyes, and climbed the stairs without calling out a hello. Once you started talking to these people, it was impossible to get away.

Roger was a very lucky raccoon. Not many freshmen were left a house and car in their great-uncle's will. Roger remembered coming here as a little kid, in the back of his folks' car. He'd liked running up and down the stairs, and sometimes there was a theater trip, or ice cream, or both. New York City had seemed so exciting, and Uncle Bob, who wore aftershave and a velvet jacket, much more glamorous than Roger's father in his suits and ties.

Then the visits stopped, though there was always a letter on Roger's birthday and at Christmas, with a few dollar bills and the instruction to spend them on something fun.

The old man must have been fonder of Roger than his great-nephew knew.

His house was handy for college—and the car, an old Plymouth station wagon, made Roger a popular guy, at least when someone wanted a ride somewhere. To cover the bills, though, he needed to rent out the second bedroom. The Village wasn't quite the place it had been when Uncle Bob moved in, and only one student responded to the flyers Roger stuck up around campus. A fox with blond hair down to the middle of his back, wearing a dress.

"It's a kaftan, man."

Roger asked him flat out if he could pay the rent.

"Hey, I will pay the rent, and I will clean the bathroom, and I will cook the meanest chili you ever tasted. And I won't interfere with your scene if you don't mess with mine, dig?"

He had mostly kept his promise about the rent and the cleaning; Roger had yet to take him up on the chili. It wasn't Frank's fault that everything he said or did drove Roger nuts.

The herbal cigarettes. The strange music he played late into the night. The way he ate Roger's food, then claimed he didn't remember doing it—bizarre items like a whole box of cereal or a package of uncooked spaghetti. Most of all, Frank's friends—strange-smelling friends in weird clothes, who liked to come round and lie on the carpet and talk disjointed nonsense for hours on end.

Creeping up his own stairs to his own bedroom in his own house so as not to disturb his uninvited guests, Roger considered his scene thoroughly interfered with.

The blind in his room was drawn to keep his books from fading in the sunlight, so it took Roger a moment to notice the naked girl in the middle of the floor.

She was sitting cross-legged, with her eyes closed and her paws held out as if she were waiting for gifts to be placed in them. Roger had never seen anything like her before. She might have been a cat, but her face was pointed like a weasel's. Her sandy fur was blotched with black. Her thick, stripy tail, which was as long again as her body, lay across her lap and up over her shoulder. In the light spilling through from the landing, she seemed to glow.

This was not something Roger felt like dealing with right now, or ever. He tiptoed backwards. But the floor creaked under his foot, and her eyes opened. They were huge, round and dark.

"Peace, man," she said.

"Er...same to you," replied Roger, his gaze fixed firmly on the ceiling.

"No, that's my name, Peace Man, I'm a linsang, it's great to meet you," she said. She was obviously used to explaining her name and species, but she sounded sincerely delighted to be doing it.

He should order her out. But it would hardly be decent to make her stand up and expose more of herself. So he should get out. But it was his room! His last refuge against the flower-powered invasion of his home!

Somehow, this particular invader didn't seem so bad. She sure smelled better than most of Frank's friends. His initial shock and bad temper were ebbing, replaced by something...fluffier?

"The scene downstairs got heavy so I came up here to

meditate." Peace Man's eyes widened. "I'm in the wrong bedroom, aren't I? You must be Roger, Frank's told us about you." She folded her arms across her chest, and her tail curled itself more tightly around her body.

"What did he say?" Roger croaked.

He regretted asking immediately. If Frank's opinion of him was anything like his own opinion of Frank, he didn't want to know. Besides, weren't there more important things he should be discussing with a naked girl in his room, if he should be discussing anything at all with her rather than, say, running away and never coming back?

"He said you're a real nice guy, but you need to loosen up a little."

"Oh." Roger had never felt more uptight in his life.

"Anyway, I'm sorry to disturb you, I'll leave you to it." She grabbed a turquoise silk shirt from behind her, slipped it on, and brushed past Roger as she made her way out of the room. That amazing tail slunk out after her; Roger watched the black tip vanish around the door jamb.

A few sandy hairs floated down to the rug. Roger, always tidy, gathered them up. There was a lingering smell of something flowery, mixed with an animal musk. He sat down heavily on the bed and massaged the dark fur above the bridge of his nose, poking at his emotions. He should be downstairs, bawling Frank out for not keeping a tighter leash on his friends. Instead, he looked at the hairs in the palm of his paw, lifted them to his nose, and sniffed gently.

"What the hell," said Roger, who never swore. "What the hell?"

Roger usually made sure his path didn't cross Frank's, but the next day he waited until he could hear the fox scrabbling around in the kitchen before making his own entrance.

"Morning," he said, which was technically true; it was five minutes to noon.

"Hey, man! Coffee's on and I'm making peanut butter toast, you want some?"

"No, thanks." Roger poured himself a mug of coffee. "Good time last night?"

Frank's ears went guilty flat.

"Peace told me what happened and I am *beyond* sorry. She didn't mean to upset you. She's a nice girl."

Just hearing Peace's name made Roger blush a little. But he'd come in here to perform an interrogation. He pressed on.

"So, have you known her long?"

Frank buttered his toast. "You're very interested in my friends all of a sudden," he said, a sly grin working along his muzzle.

When did Frank start being...perceptive? He always seemed so oblivious to everything going on around him.

"I trust your intentions towards my girl are honorable," the fox added, grinning wider.

"You and her—you're not..." Roger's heart clutched painfully.

"No, you're cool. Peace is like a sister to me. As a matter of fact I don't dig chicks, if you get me."

Roger took a step back. "Oh—I'm sorry."

"Don't be. It's a beautiful scene."

For the past semester, Roger had been living with a homosexual. This, he guessed, was the kind of danger his parents had fretted about when he moved out, although of course they had never put a precise name on their fears. He should have been horrified. Okay, he was, a little. But his first emotion was relief that Peace wasn't Frank's girlfriend.

"I don't think she's seeing anyone right now," Frank continued. When Roger didn't answer, he added "Are we cool, man? Hey, you're not gonna throw me out, are you?"

Was he? Roger wasn't sure. Could he feel comfortable sharing his home with a guy who liked other guys? But he'd already been living with him for months.

The fox's ears and tail, which usually bobbed back and forth as he grooved to whatever beat was playing in his head, were motionless, while his fingers flicked nervously.

Roger, a law student, was harbouring someone whose sexual preferences were against the law. But—the lawyer part of his brain kicked in—the fox wasn't, well, *doing* anything. If there were any acts of dreadful deviance going on in his denlike bedroom, they were very quiet ones.

Frank might be annoying, but leaving piles of dirty washing-up in the sink wasn't actually illegal—or even, Roger admitted, particularly immoral. He realized that the fox was putting an awful lot of trust in him with his confession, and he was flattered. Besides, Frank was the best chance he had of seeing Peace Man again.

"Of course not. I was just surprised, that's all."

"Thanks!"

Frank reached out to give him a hug; Roger recoiled; Frank backed off in the opposite direction. There was an awkward pause, then each held out a paw and they solemnly shook.

"It's not catching," Frank said.

"I know."

"I'd never make a move on you."

"I know."

"You're not my type."

"I—hey!"

"Sorry!" Frank laughed. "It was getting way too heavy. Anyway, I'm glad we're cool, because I, ah, I'm gonna have trouble making my rent this month."

Oh, perfect. *Perfect.* Not twenty-four hours previously, Roger would have jumped at this excuse to throw Frank out. Now that Frank was his only link to Peace, he couldn't do it. Peace? How about that for an ironic name? Roger hadn't known a moment's peace since he met her.

"I bet you've been helping out your no-good friends again," Roger said, in a tone he'd borrowed from his mom.

"My grades have slipped a bit," Frank admitted, "and the old man stopped my allowance until they improve."

"Have you considered maybe...improving them?"

"I'm on it, Roger, I swear. This semester's been kind of a bad trip for me. Just give me a month's grace to hit the books and I'll get back in my dad's good ones."

The line, and the accompanying fox grin, were so corny that Roger found himself rolling his eyes and nodding.

"Fine. You can make up the difference by doing all the cleaning," he said.

"Have a heart, Roger! What about the extra time I'll be spending in class?"

"Welcome to my world."

Roger swept out of the room, swishing his tail. It wasn't often he got one over on his canny roommate, and it felt pretty good. He headed up to the bathroom to clean his teeth. Mouth full of VOTE (the tube was squeezed in the middle, suggesting that Frank had been using it without permission), he heard a song start up on the record player downstairs, at wall-shaking volume. Since he was unable to voice his usual *Hey, keep it down!*, he stomped hard on the floor with one foot.

The floorboards gave a wet crack, and a large section fell away in rotten splinters to leave a beachball-sized hole. Drops of water spattered down. Cables fizzed. Roger yanked his foot out of the way and balanced on one leg while he took stock of the disaster. Frank appeared in the doorway, his fur white with plaster dust and his tail puffed out like a popcorn ball.

"Missed me by *that* much," he reported.

"Now what are we going to do? I don't just take your rent to be mean, Frank—I need it for emergencies like this."

Frank's tail deflated and tucked itself between his legs. "Sorry I'm such a flake."

"It's not your fault the ceiling fell in." Roger peered through the hole to the mess below. "How about making a start on your promise to keep this place clean?"

"Sure, Roger. Right away, Roger."

As the fox scampered off, Roger puzzled over his suspicious eagerness to obey. Was he really feeling that guilty about the rent? Maybe. The raccoon knelt by the tub, looking for the cause of the problem. Must have been a pretty big damp patch to cause a cave-in like that. A leak in the tank, perhaps. He got down on paws and knees to investigate the space under the eaves, behind the tub, where the bathroom ceiling sloped down to meet the floor.

What the heck? Ranged in the small space under the roof, sunbathing under their own little lamp, were three rows of bushy plants with skinny, jagged leaves like outstretched fingers. Rather than earth, their roots rested in tanks of water. But the third tank was almost empty, the plants drooping, and a dark wet patch spread from it across the floor.

"So it *was* your fault," Roger said under his breath.

"Hydroponics, man!" Frank announced when Roger challenged him downstairs. He had a dustpan and brush in his paws already. "Growing plants without soil! It's the future!"

"*Your* future is looking pretty goddamn bleak," Roger threatened. Even as he said it, he regretted the ridiculous *goddamn*. Sure enough, the corners of Frank's muzzle twitched upwards.

"Ooh! Heavy!" he said, bugging out his eyes. "Sorry. Sorry, Roger. It's not funny, I goofed, and I'm going to fix it, okay? Just trust me."

Roger was skeptical, but he had little choice. He could always ask his parents for help, of course, but that would mean a lecture from his mom about not saving for a rainy day. Then his dad would want to come and inspect the work to make sure it was done properly, and his mom would come along for the ride, and the precious independence he'd built up for himself would be shattered. Frank would laugh at him, and Roger found to his surprise that he cared. He cared, too, about the idea of his folks seeing Frank's beanbags and candles and the posters in his room and the *dress*—no use telling them it was called a kaftan—and thinking their only son was living among freaks. His living situation was none of their business. Uncle Bob had passed the house down to him, not them...

"Hello in there!" Frank was waving a paw in front of his eyes. "You want to go see Peace tonight? She's playing at this coffee shop in the Village. I know it's not your usual scene, but she's pretty good."

Tonight? Roger wasn't sure he was ready. He wasn't sure he'd be ready in a week, a month or a decade...in which case, tonight was as good a time as any.

"Sure," he said. "I'll get some studying in first. Maybe you'd better do the same—when you've cleaned up down here."

"Got some good news on the academic front," Frank reported.

"Oh yeah?"

"The ceiling apocalypse scenario took out the old boob tube, so I'll have a *lot* more time to study."

"The boob...you mean the TV? Aww, *Frank!*"

"I don't want to tell you how to do your thing, man, but could you maybe lose the tie?"

Roger's paw went defensively to his collar. "My mother gave me this!"

"Yeah...it kinda shows."

"Fine."

Roger took off his tie and laid it carefully across the back of a chair, then undid the top button of his shirt.

"Let's go," he said.

He still felt overdressed in the dark little coffee shop. Shirts were being worn open in the Village this season, or not worn at all. Fur was unkempt and hair was long. One guy seemed to be wearing nothing but a large flag, with holes cut for his head and tail. Roger was pretty sure that counted as desecration.

On the stage, a goat in a black turtleneck was speaking into a microphone. None of his words, when Roger could make them out at all, seemed to make the slightest bit of sense, so he guessed it was a poetry recital. Some of the other customers were gazing at him, rapt, while others flat out ignored the performance. Roger decided to join the latter camp.

An Old English Sheepdog came over to their table, his eyes invisible under his woolly hair.

"Hey! Frank!"

"Davy! Hi! This is Roger."

Frank stood and moved towards the sheepdog, who gave a tiny shake of his head and backed up, with a jerk of his muzzle towards Roger.

"He's cool," Frank said. Roger was? Cool with what? *Ohh.*

"It's okay," Roger confirmed. He stared fixedly at the singer. Out of the corner of his eye, he saw the sheepdog give Frank's ear an affectionate nip before the two sat down together. Their shoulders touched, and Roger suspected they were holding paws under the table.

It didn't make Roger feel any more uncomfortable than he already did. But that wasn't saying much.

The goat stalked off the stage, to be replaced by a massive brown bear who sang on one note in a rumbling bass. Roger couldn't make out the words, but his coffee cup vibrated on its saucer.

Frank nudged him. "Stick around. Seriously," he said. "You've got a treat coming."

At last, Peace stepped into the ring of light. Roger had been starting to think he'd maybe misremembered the way she looked, if he hadn't dreamed her entire existence, but picked out by the spotlight her fur looked even softer and more golden, her dark eyes more liquid and mysterious, than they had last night. She sat cross-legged on the stool, lifted her guitar to her lap and spoke into the microphone.

"Hi. This is called 'Song for Joe'."

She could have performed the Alphabet Song in the style of a hyena with laryngitis and Roger would still have been spellbound. But Frank had been right—she was good.

"Sometimes I see you in the corner of my eye
But when I turn around it's just a shadow.
Sometimes I think I hear you laugh that way you did
But it's always just the wind across the meadow.
Life is a one-way track
The light turns green and there's no going back
But if I could
Then I would
And I'd be with you."

She had a low, clear voice, and her claws picked the strings softly. She played a set of four songs, then stood up, acknowledged the audience's finger-snapping and claw-clicking with a wave, and walked out of the light.

A couple of minutes later she appeared at their table, minus her guitar and wearing a fresh shirt.

"Great set, doll." Frank stood up. "Davy and I are heading to the club. Why don't you hang out with Roger for a while?"

"Sure. Be careful," Peace said, kissing Frank on the cheek.

It was the most sisterly of pecks, but it still made Roger so jealous that in an earlier era he would have ripped Frank's throat out with his teeth.

"And don't call me 'doll'," Peace called after them. She sat down beside the raccoon.

"Don't you want to go with them?" Roger asked.

"It's kind of a special club, where they can be themselves. Besides, I'd rather stay and talk to you."

She'd rather stay and talk to him? Heaven!

Unfortunately, he seemed to have forgotten how to talk. "I liked your songs," he managed eventually.

"Thank you."

"Would you like a coffee?"

"No thanks."

Stop saying 'like', Roger told himself. *You're, like, starting to sound like Frank.*

Peace fidgeted. "Roger—it's late and that was a tiring set, so..."

He didn't want to lose her now. He hadn't done much so far to prove he was a fun companion, but he had to try.

"Can I walk you home?"

Her eyes twinkled with mischief. "Sure. That would be lovely."

After the first block her paw slipped into his. Surprised, Roger flicked his tail, which caught Peace across the buttocks.

Before he could apologize, her own long and sinuous tail wound around him and draped across his shoulder like a scarf.

Roger stroked it with his free paw as they walked. She was so relaxed with him that he became less jittery himself, easing into this new feeling of togetherness.

Out in the fresh air, away from the noise and smoke, Roger found his tongue. He talked about his law degree, his fussy mother, Uncle Bob's house and how come Frank lived there with him. Peace didn't seem impressed at Roger's possession of a house and car, but she laughed at his Frank stories, so he worked on those until it sounded like life with the fox was a real laugh-in.

Although she'd been chatty the night before, Peace seemed content to listen and smile. She didn't say much about herself, except that she had come across from China with her parents when she was a baby. Her first memory was of being held up to the ship's rail to look at the moonlight on the sea.

"What's yours?" she asked.

Roger thought about it. "I remember my mom baking cupcakes," he said. That was long, long ago—when his parents were his whole world. The feel and scent of her pink apron came vividly back to him. "She told me not to touch the ingredients, but I sneaked a big spoonful of baking soda, because if it goes in cakes it has to taste good, right? It didn't."

Peace just laughed and squeezed his paw.

"Well, this is me," she said at last.

Roger looked up. They were standing in front of the coffee shop again.

The linsang was giggling. "I rent the room upstairs. Are you mad at me?"

She had deliberately led him around in a circle for half an hour. Half an hour of her delightful company, which he wouldn't have had otherwise. How could Roger get mad about that? He started to laugh.

"Want to come in for a drink?" Her paw looped round his waist.

"I ought to be getting home. Early class tomorrow," he said. "But I'd like to see you again. Very much."

"What are you doing in the afternoon?"

"Er...nothing." Studying. Working on his paper. Who cared?

"Let's go for a walk in the park. I'll meet you by the gate. Two?"

The word had a magical ring to Roger. For him, it meant not just two o'clock in the afternoon but two of them. Roger and Peace. Two-gether.

Too corny?

"Two," he said.

The linsang made no move to go indoors. Instead, she took hold of his tie and gently tugged, so the raccoon's face was drawn closer to her own.

He reached up and put a paw on each of her spotted cheeks. The fur was soft, and he could feel the warmth of her beneath it. It would be okay, right, to give her a kiss? It was the gentlemanly thing to do after escorting a lady home. He...

Before he could finish the thought, Peace pressed her muzzle against his and kissed him.

Turn On

Roger carried the memory of that kiss with him through the next morning's classes. The way Peace's whiskers had tickled his chin. Her tiny, sharp teeth and the taste of her mouth, sweet with a slight bitter edge of coffee. The way they had held the clinch, and each other. Roger, reluctantly, withdrew first, and Peace's "Goodnight!" was a whispered giggle as she disappeared into her doorway...

"You look happy," observed his friend Brian from the next desk.

"Mmmm."

"Want to grab some lunch after this?"

"Sorry, Bry. I've...I'm meeting someone."

Brian was a neatly-dressed, soft-spoken puma; the sort of person Roger's mother would have labeled a Nice Boy. He played hockey and football and was on the debating team.

"Someone nice? Do tell!"

Roger wasn't sure he should open up about this new, strange part of his life to Brian, but he found he wanted to tell someone.

So he told everything, from finding Peace behind his bedroom door to kissing her goodnight. Brian's eyes grew round.

"A real hippie chick! I've heard about them!"

So had Roger. "She's not like that," he snapped, curling his paws into fists.

"Oops. Sorry. You really like her, huh?"

Roger nodded. Yes. He really did like her.

At ten to two, he was standing by the park gate with a bunch of violets in his paw.

At five to two, he was nervous.

At two, he was trying to look casual.

At five past, he was worried.

At ten past, he was almost tearful.

At 2:15, Peace Man came running across the grass and threw herself into his arms.

"Hey!" she said. "Am I late? I don't have a watch. Are these for me? Nobody's ever brought me flowers before. Where would you like to go? How about over by the trees? Come on!"

Dazed, Roger let Peace take his paw and lead him through the park. Wandering in and out of the dappled sunlight, past beds of bright pink and purple flowers, he wondered if he was dreaming.

He didn't wake up. He didn't even suddenly realize that he was out in public with no pants on, which usually happened in his dreams.

"So," Roger said as they ate ice cream, "when can I see you again?" He'd never dated before, not really, but he had a vague idea it was something that happened once a week, like grocery shopping.

Peace wrinkled her nose as she considered. "How about tomorrow?"

Tomorrow, and the next day, and the one after that. Roger and Peace sat holding hands outside coffee shops, or in the intimate dark of the movie house. They walked around the Village—Peace knew every street, and Roger saw some pretty strange sights, but he couldn't be shocked or afraid with Peace's soft paw in his.

The other part of his life, the college part, slipped into a twilit shadow spent dreaming of the Peace times in between.

Now he was seeing the world through the linsang's eyes, he even started to get on better with Frank and his strange friends. He learned to tell them apart, so they became individuals rather than the ungroomed, smelly mass he had always perceived before. Ungroomed, smelly individuals perhaps, but individuals nonetheless.

Moon was the motherly jackrabbit, and Weird was the coyote with the pale, mad-looking eyes. Tom and Anna, a cat couple, spent most of their time entwined, Tom's black tail wrapped around Anna's white one and their lips pressed together. They didn't say much; most of the time, talking would have been a physical impossibility. The others talked. About the war in Asia, about music, about stuff Roger didn't understand, dropping names and words he didn't know: *square, groove, peacenik, freak; Zappa, Garfunkel, Dylan.*

And of course there was Davy, the sheepdog, Frank's boyfriend. He came to the house much more often now Roger knew Frank's preference. Frank and Davy held paws in the living-room, looking about as far out and freaky as a couple of loving grandparents.

It took Roger longer to get used to the way Peace would flop down with her head on Frank's lap and her feet against Moon's leg. Roger himself still suffered agonies of shyness every time he reached for Peace's paw or kissed her face, and he was often consumed with crazy jealousy of Frank and all his friends for the easy intimacy they shared with his girlfriend. That was the only flaw in his rainbow bubble.

Well, that and the bathroom floor. Frank came home one night with a metal road sign that said SPEED LIMIT 50 and duct-taped it over the hole, but it was hardly a long-term solution, besides presumably being stolen State property.

But Peace was his girlfriend. That was the important thing. He was the one she stayed up all night with, the light from the scented candles making her face mysterious and alluring. In the early morning she would dance out into the sunlit street while Roger prepared himself for another day of sleepwalking through class.

With Frank and the others she talked for hours about nothing. With Roger, she talked for hours about everything. Not the global stuff—they stayed off politics, and the Asian war—but hopes and fears and dreams. Stuff Roger hadn't thought he could ever tell another person.

They were sitting up late one evening, drinking cheap red wine from mugs in Peace's tiny room above the coffee shop. Peace didn't have any chairs so they both sat on the bed, which to Roger still seemed thrillingly intimate.

"Want to hear a song I'm working on?" Peace asked. Although she was happy to perform for a shop full of people, she was shy about her music in front of Roger and didn't offer often. Roger nodded and leaned back, placing a cushion between his head and the wall.

He watched her slim, black fingers move across the strings, and peeped at the adorable way her forehead creased and the tip of her tongue poked out when she was concentrating. Her tail swayed with the rhythm; when she played a quick, lively tune it twitched and jerked, when the music went sad and slow it rippled gently from side to side.

There were no words yet, but Peace hummed a melody, changing and correcting it as she went along. Roger was tapping his knees with his paws, totally unaware he was doing so.

"That's it, now you're in the groove!" laughed Peace, laying down her guitar. Roger jumped.

"Sorry! I didn't realize!"

"You looked sweet. I'm glad you feel my music."

"I wish I was creative like you," Roger said, examining the back of his paw.

"You're smarter than me," Peace said.

Roger didn't deny this. "I can't imagine you tapping out a beat to my essay on *habeas corpus*."

"We should try," Peace giggled. "It might be a turn-on!"

Roger's arm went round her shoulders. "You're a turn-on," he told her, emboldened by the wine. It was a corny line, but Peace laughed and snuggled up against him.

"I was studying music in college," she told him suddenly, "but I dropped out. Too many rules. I just wanted to make music, not learn hundreds of years of history and theory."

"Oh, Peace, you should go back! You're clever and talented—college will help you get on in life!" Roger sat up, his passions stirred.

"That's what my folks said," Peace replied.

There was a short silence. Something had come between them, and Roger shivered with it. He put his paw on the bare, spotted knee.

"Sorry," he said.

Gradually the linsang relaxed and her ruffled fur lay back down. Her dark eyes closed. Roger leaned down and kissed her forehead, then moved on to the mouth.

Peace reached up and grabbed his ears, pulling him towards her. At the same time she swung her legs onto the bed, so Roger was lying on top of her.

Roger pressed down on her mouth, exploring the sharp little teeth with his tongue. Her hands twined behind his back, untucking his shirt from his pants and massaging the nubs of his spine. She scritched at his ribs and squeezed the little rolls of flesh at his sides. Then she worked her way round to the front.

She paused with her fingers on his belt buckle, tugging at it slightly so Roger was drawn closer to her. Her mouth tickled against his ear.

"I'm on the Pill," she whispered.

For a moment, he didn't know what she meant. His first thought was that she was sick, his next that she was addicted to some drug and needed his help. Then the realization of what she meant, and why she'd told him, hit him like a cartoon hammer.

He knelt astride the linsang, lifted her up and buried his muzzle in her neck. She held on to him, letting him take her weight, and squeaked softly.

"You're tickling," she laughed. "So...do you want to?"

"More than anything," Roger confessed, "but I..."

He knew that what he was about to say would mark him out as an A-1 square, and Peace would probably never want anything to do with him ever again. Nevertheless, he had to say it.

"I'm not ready." He swallowed. "I always assumed I'd wait until I was married, and now I'm not sure, but now, tonight, it's too soon."

Peace smiled at him. "You're old-fashioned," she said, "and sweet."

Roger's relief was so great that he kissed her again.

"Stay here tonight?" she asked. "I just mean to sleep. You can sleep on the floor, or I'll have the floor and you can take the bed, or...or you can come in with me."

Roger might have been square but he wasn't made of stone. He slept in Peace's bed, in his T-shirt and briefs, with the linsang spooned against him.

In the morning he crept out without waking her; she would be working at the coffeehouse later, and performing later still.

To his surprise, when he reached home Frank was up and about, preparing to make one of his rare forays into college.

"Night on the tiles, huh?" he said knowingly, a foxy smile sneaking up his muzzle.

"Not like that!" Roger snapped. "She's a good girl."

Frank nodded. "Got it. You hitting campus? I'll walk with you."

Roger couldn't exactly refuse, although showing up with Frank, who this morning was sporting a red-and-green outfit that made him look like a jester at a medieval court, would not improve his standing among the law students. He was far from spruce himself, though, in yesterday's shirt, and somehow it didn't seem to matter very much. He didn't have time to go up and wash, nor did he feel up to navigating the bathroom floor. Knowing how little separated him from the drop to the room below—and from its occupants, when Frank was holding court— he'd taken to showering at the gym on campus.

"Having sex doesn't make you a bad person."

They had been silent for most of the walk, and Frank's sudden speech made Roger jump.

"You're going to need to understand that if you're going to hang out with me and my friends. And that includes Peace," the fox continued. "There's nothing wicked or dirty about making love. It's a beautiful thing."

"I didn't say it wasn't," said Roger, sulkily. "I just...want to wait a while. I think."

"Then that's your scene, and I won't judge it, even though I think you might be missing out on some wonderful stuff. But you shouldn't judge others either, unless your scene is judging others, and that's not a good scene, you dig?"

Roger was beginning to understand Frank's world. Everyone should be free to live their life as they pleased—but you didn't necessarily have to like it. It was certainly much simpler than the tangle of legal procedure Roger was studying. Speaking of which...

"I'm going this way. The English faculty is over there," he said helpfully, since it had been so long since Frank's last appearance on campus.

Frank stuck his tongue out at his roomie, and for a second they were a couple of cubs horsing around at recess.

"See you tonight?"

"Yeah. See you!"

Roger was trying to write a paper.

He was *trying* to write a paper.

He was TRYING to WRITE a PAPER.

It wasn't that the noise drifting across the landing from Frank's room was particularly loud, by Frank's standards at least. It was even reasonably tuneful, not like that awful one last night with the screechy bits that had made the raccoon's tail fluff up like cotton candy. It was just that he had *told* Frank time and time again to keep his *door* shut if he *had* to listen to music. Roger didn't see how the fox could possibly study with that ruckus going on, if indeed he was studying, he'd get his tail thrown out of college if he wasn't careful, but why should Roger care, who was he, Frank's mom?

Gradually, Roger became aware that his teeth were clenched together and his left paw had scrunched the first page of his paper into a ball. It had been mostly White-Out anyway, but he was still annoyed.

His feet, however, hadn't got the memo about being annoyed, because they were twitching under his desk in time to the beat. Somehow, this made Roger madder than ever. He hopped off his chair, marched across the landing into Frank's den, and threw the crumpled paper ball at the back of the fox's head.

Frank would have fallen off his beanbag, if such a feat were physically possible. He jumped and slumped further down before rolling to his feet.

"Hey, roomie," he grinned, "is this a duel? Because I'm into peace and stuff, but I can cream you in a paper fight. Words are my weapon, after all."

"Will you turn that..." Then Roger tailed off, because, speaking of Peace, she was curled on Frank's rug, under the curtained window. "Peace! What are you doing here?"

"She's a free spirit," Frank said.

The linsang sat up. "Hi, Roger."

Roger could tell from her voice that the linsang wasn't feeling her normal, happy self. But why had she come to Frank first, rather than him, Roger, her boyfriend? He bubbled with jealousy like a lava lamp bubbles with...with...whatever they put in lava lamps. The feeling was quickly replaced with paranoia: maybe she was unhappy with *him*, and that was why she was hanging out with his roommate. His roommate who, after all, liked other guys, so there was no need for Roger to panic.

"I didn't know you were here," he said, walking over to give her a hug. Peace lifted her arms and pulled him down beside her.

"You had the Do Not Disturb sign up," she said.

"That only applies to Frank," Roger told her.

"Hey, that's Frankist," the fox complained. "That's blatant Frankism, man. It borders on Frankophobia."

Roger wasn't listening. He often didn't listen to Frank, but this time it was because Peace had her skinny arms locked around Roger's back and her face smushed into his chest. She wrapped her long, lovely tail around them both, her perfume drowning out the smell of fox and incense and unvacuumed carpet. She wasn't crying, but she wasn't far off it.

"Since the chick's not talking," Frank broke into Roger's moment, "I may as well tell you. The coffee shop's closing. Some breadhead developer's bought the land."

Peace lifted her muzzle from Roger's shirt front to say "Don't call me a chick, Frank, how many times?"

"Sorry, doll."

Roger opened his mouth to tell Frank to get out, then remembered it was Frank's bedroom.

"Want to get a..." He tripped over the word 'coffee' and corrected it to 'tea'. Peace nodded and followed him downstairs, her paw tucked into his.

Peace was silent as Roger fussed with the teapot, a gift from his mother and seldom used. Measuring the loose tea, he thought hard. If the coffee shop closed, Peace would have no job and no place to go. Maybe she could sleep on his couch? Frank would be okay with that, at least he better be, but it still seemed a little forward.

The idea of inviting Peace to share his own bedroom was, of course, unthinkable. He accidentally thought of it anyway, and his paw trembled so much he spilled tea across the table.

The tea didn't end up exactly like his mother's, but he'd never liked his mother's tea. Peace seemed to think it was okay, curling her paws around the cup and smiling over it at Roger. He opened a package of Fudge Town cookies and suddenly Frank was in the kitchen with them, though Roger hadn't heard the stairs creak. Spooky, the way the fox always showed up when there was food.

"So," Roger said, taking charge. "What's the plan?"

Peace perked up. "We're having a sit-in!" she said.

"What's a sit-in?"

"We, like, *sit*," Frank explained patiently, "*in* the coffee shop."

"Oh. And that's going to help, is it?"

"We'll sing protest songs," Peace continued.

"The chick's already on it," said Frank. If Peace noticed the 'chick', she was too excited to care.

"Frank's helping," Peace said. "You can, too! You're good with words!"

"Songs? Sitting? How's that going to help?" Roger ran his fingers through the fur on his head. "No, no, no. We need a proper legal defense. I'll read up on the local property laws, go through the fine print, and put a case together." He cracked his knuckles.

"Fine, man, be like that," Frank said. "You just don't believe in the power of music...the power of the *people*. That's cool. That's your scene. Glad it's not mine."

He stuffed three cookies into his muzzle and huffed out.

"What's biting *him*?" Roger asked.

"Something to do with Davy, I think," Peace said. "They were going to a show together, but Davy had to work."

"What does that guy do, anyway? Not many sheep to herd in NYC."

The linsang didn't laugh.

"Peace? You see what I mean, don't you? That the law's going to be worth more than some song about flowers?"

"I just want to do something," she said, folding back her ears. "I'm not clever like you. I'm not a law major. All I have is my voice."

"It's a wonderful voice, Peace. You've got a real talent."

"Thanks for the tea."

She kissed him and slipped away. Frank always showed up when he was least welcome; Peace always vanished when Roger wanted her most.

Tune In

The flow of strangely-dressed and often pungent-smelling people in and out of Roger's house increased over the next few days, while his icebox and cupboards emptied. The raccoon never knew what he would find when he peeped timidly into his own living-room. Sometimes they held paws in a circle, lit by candles; at other times they might be painting Day-Glo slogans on signboards, or onto each other's fur. As long as they didn't make a mess of the carpet, he decided to let them be.

He couldn't escape the music, however. It started up late in the evening and continued into the night, occasionally into Roger's dreams. He could make out Frank's guitar, strumming constantly behind all the other sounds as the fox tried out chords. The muffled, regular tapping was Moon the jackrabbit, on the drum she called a *tabla* and beat with her paws, while the mournful wail that made the fur on Roger's neck stand on end was the milky-eyed coyote, Weird, playing his harmonica. Weaving in and out of the music were the voices—the laughter, the singing, the cheers and the long, whooping calls.

It was easy for Roger to identify Peace's voice among the

others; to him, it always sounded the clearest and the sweetest, like a sparrow among crows. When he heard her soaring laugh, Roger himself felt more like a snail, tied to the ground, and he pulled the pillow over his ears.

Peace asked him several times to join in, to help with the lyrics and to sing, but he always shook his head. He had made his position clear and he didn't want to back down. Besides, he was shy about his singing voice, especially in front of all those strangers. Lying in bed, he felt as far removed from the circle downstairs as if he was inside one of the Apollo rockets up in space. It all sounded like noise to him, yet sometimes he'd find himself humming a strand of the melody they were making.

Usually, to his embarrassment, while he was in class.

Roger kept his promise to help in his own way. He spent as much time as possible at the library, or sometimes lugged books on property law home with him. He researched the history of the coffee shop and the neighborhood, made copious notes, and put together a case. His plan was to meet with the developer, a guy named Brennan with his paws in property all over the city, and present his argument. It might even be worth extra credit.

But then he would have to explain how come he'd got interested in a hippie hangout. Maybe he should keep the whole thing extracurricular.

Roger focused on the small paw holding his. It stopped him thinking too much about everything else going on around him. The linsang's claws pricked his palm as they extended and retracted, and Roger guessed she was nervous. Under his other arm he clutched Peace's guitar case, which he had, of course, offered to carry. It made him feel like an old-time gangster, but something told him that wouldn't be a popular opinion among this bunch. Peace's friends wore flowers in their fur. Some of them wore little else. Several sported dyed or shaved patches. He even thought he glimpsed the long white tresses of his elderly otter neighbor. They all thronged in front of the coffee shop, waving their signs and cheering. It was like a circus.

"Where's Frank?" Roger didn't usually miss having his roomie around, but it would have been nice to have the devil he knew to act as a barrier between himself and all these devils he didn't.

"Back at your pad, waiting for Davy. I hope he doesn't flake out—I need his rhythm guitar."

"What's rhythm guitar?"

"The lead guitar picks out the tune and the rhythm sort of strums along in the background, holding it all together." Peace fluttered her paws, demonstrating.

That sounded like Frank, all right: the constant chord behind the varying notes of his friends' noise. Roger took Peace's paw again; the last thing he wanted was to lose her in this crowd.

"There's Moon!" Peace pulled him over to the jackrabbit, who was kneeling on the sidewalk as she applied face paint to the smallest in a family of mice. She held up a mirror to show her client the rainbow on his forehead and the butterfly on each cheek, and the toddler giggled delightedly.

"Roger! You made it!" Moon stood and stretched. "Want me to make you up?"

"No thanks," Roger smiled.

"Hey, the press are here!"

Roger looked beyond the brightly-coloured crowd to where a second crowd had gathered, watching. In their ordinary clothes, they looked drab and colourless. Some of them wore cameras round their necks or carried notepads, and were obviously The Press, while others were simply rubbernecking. People with nothing better to do, like tourists and students.

Students. Including some of Roger's classmates. He spun round to face the other way.

"Moon? I think I will have my face done, after all."

The jackrabbit beamed and got to work.

"Close your eyes," she instructed, and Roger felt the gentle strokes of a paintbrush across his eyelids. A paw on his shoulder held him still. He could smell Peace beside him, and a couple of times he heard her giggle.

"Done!"

Roger looked in the little mirror, and chuckled. His left eye was surrounded by a yellow sunburst, his right by a blue crescent moon, and glittery stars sprinkled his dark muzzle. The chances of any of his classmates recognising him now were slim.

"You look..."

Roger waited for Peace's verdict. Groovy? Fab? Far out? Some new expression he hadn't yet heard?

"Cute," the linsang concluded. Then she flashed him a nervous smile and unlatched her guitar case.

The strap slung around her neck, she spent a few moments tuning the strings, one ear held close to the instrument. She played a few bars before beginning to sing quietly. Moon joined in, louder, and the song rippled outwards through the crowd until there were dozens of voices carrying the melody. It was simple and powerful; Roger could imagine an army chanting it as they marched, sweeping all before them.

He already knew the tune—he had heard it floating up the stairs enough times—and by the second chorus he found he knew the words, too. He felt himself swaying from side to side, and realised his lips were moving, although no sound emerged. He felt a paw round his waist and saw Moon there, smiling and singing. The jackrabbit had a loud voice and missed a few high notes, but she was so completely unselfconscious about it, and drowned out the singers around her so successfully, that Roger took courage, and a breath, and suddenly he was joining in. Little lights sprang up like fireflies in the dusk, illuminating floaty, tie-dyed kaftans and glittering eyes. It took Roger a while to realise the magic flames were Zippos. Whenever the song started to die, someone somewhere in the crowd picked it up again from the beginning.

Roger was starting to wonder when it would end—his feet hurt, and he was thirsty. His answer came with the shrill blast of a police whistle. The edges of the crowd were shifting and billowing like shingle on a beach, as a wave of blue-clad figures broke upon it again and again.

Roger held Peace against him so he wouldn't lose her, while the linsang clutched her guitar tight. Placards swayed and fell like chopped trees, and the solid mass of people broke up into knots and clusters. Some ran. Some fought.

"We weren't doing anything," she yelled up into his ear. "We were just singing!"

"I know," Roger shouted back, struggling to keep his feet. "Stay still!"

Someone toppled into Roger, and he staggered. Peace tried to hold him but someone else grabbed her from the other side—whether trying to help or hurt, Roger couldn't tell. In the confusion, the red bikini top she wore was torn from her chest and trampled underfoot.

Peace shrieked and wrapped her arms around her chest. Not quite as free and easy as she appeared, then, Roger thought. But already he was pulling his shirt off like Superman, buttons popping, so he could lay it across his girlfriend's bare, spotted shoulders while carefully averting his eyes. Peace snuggled into the shirt, and darted a quicksilver kiss across his muzzle. Pretty soon it didn't matter how many clothes Peace was wearing; the press of the crowd was too thick, as the police corralled them into a smaller and smaller circle. Roger's legs felt wobbly, and Peace's breathing was fast and panicky. What would Moon do?

"Chill out, Peace," he said, moving his thumb in a circle between her shoulder blades. She was carrying her tail high so it wouldn't get stepped on. Now she coiled it tightly around them both.

"Don't like feeling trapped," she whispered.

"I've got you. You're safe." Could they drop to all fours and crawl to freedom? Roger looked wildly around.

"Rogeeeeer!"

The raccoon looked up. An Econoline van he recognised as Weird's was careering down the street, resplendent in its green and purple paint job. Police and civilians alike parted before its crazy path and two-tone horn, and the coyote at the wheel with his black leather vest and silver earrings. The passenger door was hanging open and Frank leaned out, waving.

Roger lifted Peace up in his arms. She scrambled up onto his shoulders and sprang for the van, Roger's shirt flapping from her back. Frank caught her and hauled her in.

Even as he admired her amazing leap and the sight of her body in flight, Roger was pushing and elbowing his own way towards rescue. The van slowed to a crawl and Roger held out his paws to Frank, who helped him inside. Peace, in the middle of the front seat, made room for him by perching on his lap.

"Hi, I'm Weird and I will be your spirit guide today. Next stop: *out there!*" Weird proclaimed around his cigarette. Roger was so pleased to see him, he didn't even ask to open a window.

"Where *were* you?" Roger yelled as soon as the front door closed behind them. Yelling at Frank was unfair, and he knew it, but he had to yell at someone and it wasn't going to be Peace. Frank cringed and looked away, his ears flicking like crazy.

"It's okay, Frank..." Peace began.

"It's not okay!" The fox wouldn't meet their eyes. "Davy

came over and we...we were making out. I say making out, but it was all kinds of stuff I'd never done before. Stuff I can't tell you about, Roger, or you'll throw me out."

Roger rolled his eyes, but managed not to say anything.

"I kept saying we had to leave or we'd miss the protest"—Frank had a sense of time? A conscience? This was news to Roger—"but every time I opened my muzzle he, he kissed me. I mean, my knees were trembling, it was..."

"We get it, thanks."

"No, Roger, you don't. Because at last I said that was enough, we really had to get our act together. And that's when he told me. He'd had a tipoff about the police raid and he wanted to keep me safe. I kinda lost my cool with him, told him my loyalty was with my friends and I oughta be down there getting my head kicked in right beside you. I chewed him out for not telling me straight away so I could warn you and then I came right over, but I was too late." He smacked the side of his own head. "I was thinking with my pants, man."

"That's all right," Roger found himself saying. "I've been talking through mine. I didn't think there was any point to singing and playing the guitar, and...it was wonderful. Just amazing."

Peace, still enveloped in Roger's shirt, wound her arm around his and slipped her paw in his pants pocket. Roger could tell just from the slack feel of her fur how downhearted she was.

"It didn't work, though, did it? We just got chased off. You were right and I was wrong."

"I'll go see Brennan tomorrow and see if I have better luck," Roger promised, without correcting her. "Now let's get out of here."

When he finally closed his eyes in bed that night, Roger could still feel the stiff spikes of paint in the fur around them. He could see the swaying crowd and hear their song. It was so pretty, so full of passion. Shame it couldn't achieve anything.

The reception area at Brennan Incorporated was all light wood and glass. Roger, feeling small in a vast Naugahyde chair, picked up one of the brochures fanned across the glass surface of the coffee table. Within its pages, gleaming office blocks thrust up towards an impossibly blue and clear New York sky.

Roger had entered like a knight braving the dragon's lair. He was dressed in his armour of freshly-ironed white shirt, navy blue suit and his college tie, and was already sweltering on this mild spring morning. Now he waited, meekly. He finished his brochure and picked up another. He checked his watch, an eighteenth birthday present from his parents. He fiddled with his tie.

One way or another, he reflected, he was always waiting for Peace.

He tapped his fingers on the coffee table, stopping abruptly when he saw the smears his pads had made on the glass. He wiped the table with his handkerchief. This would not do. Time to face that dragon. He extracted himself from the chair and walked over to the desk.

The receptionist, a Siamese cat, favored him with a smile. "Yes?"

"I'm here to see Mr Breadhead—I mean Brennan." *Darn you, Frank!*

She opened a desk diary. "What time is your appointment?"

"An hour ago."

The Siamese picked up the phone on her desk and dialled with a claw painted pink to match her blouse. She spoke in a low purr Roger couldn't catch. The response was a bark that made her wince and move the receiver further from her ear.

"Mr Brennan is a very busy fox," she said, apologetically. "Can I get you a coffee?"

As Roger was passing the paper cup from paw to paw to keep from burning himself, an elderly gray fox in a suit a couple shades darker than his fur swished through Reception and out to a long, black car idling outside, adjusting the tilt of his trilby as he went.

"Lunch. Hold my calls," he snapped at the receptionist.

Roger jumped up, boiling coffee narrowly missing his pants leg.

"Was that Mr Brennan?" he asked the cat, already knowing the answer.

"He's a very busy fox," she said again, raising an eyebrow.

Roger didn't know what else to do, so he stayed. He wouldn't have minded some lunch himself but he didn't want Brennan to sneak back in while he was gone.

Brennan returned precisely fifty-nine minutes after he left. As he strode past Roger, he shot the raccoon a look. "Are you coming or not? I'm a very busy fox!"

He swept into the elevator, Roger just making it in after him before the doors closed.

Still in Brennan's slipstream, Roger found himself walking into an office decorated in dark wood. It was more old-fashioned than the reception area, but one wall was mostly window, giving an impressive view of the skyline. Brennan dropped into the padded swivel chair behind his desk. Roger took the seat opposite.

The gray fox steepled his fingers. "Well, young man, what do you have for me?"

Roger laid his file on the desk and launched into his piece. Brennan listened with apparent interest, nodding his head at appropriate moments. Roger gained confidence and gathered steam, running through the historical and social significance of the little group of shops threatened by the new development. He pointed a claw at documents and blueprints Xeroxed at the law library. He was no longer a law student. He was an *orator*.

He could tell his speech wasn't succeeding, though. Brennan had the look of someone who is about, reluctantly, to puncture a bubble.

From the street below, Roger heard a single guitar string, and the chord that answered it. Lead and rhythm. Brennan's ears swivelled.

Roger pressed on, but it was clear he no longer had the gray fox's full attention. As other instruments and voices joined to create a familiar melody, Roger began to lose the thread of his presentation, and stuttered to a stop.

Brennan rose from his desk, presumably to tell Roger he should stop wasting his time and get out. Instead, the director moved over to the window. Roger hesitated, then joined him.

A flash of rainbow colors down at pavement level. On the sidewalk outside the building, blocking the entrance, sat a mass of hippies. Away from their natural surroundings, among the people in their businesswear and the gray, square buildings, they looked brighter and more startling than they had at the coffee shop. Somewhere in the crowd, Roger thought he saw a long, sinuous tail bobbing, and the swish of a kaftan around the body of a tall, lean fox.

"Is this...activity something to do with you?" asked Brennan.

"I think it might be, sir," Roger admitted. The aircon made the fine hairs of his tail billow behind him.

Brennan stalked back to his desk and flicked through the pages of Roger's file. "What was that address again?" he muttered. "Well! Why didn't you *say* so?" He banged the file shut. "The acquisition was made by one of my directors. I was unaware of its location. Property developers are not necessarily breadheads, Mr..."

"Jones," Roger supplied.

"Jones?" Brennan glanced sharply up at that and looked straight at Roger for the first time. His gaze stayed on the raccoon's face for a long time, as if he was taking careful note of every detail. "No relation to Robert Jones, I suppose?" he asked at last.

"My great-uncle."

"Bob Jones's great-nephew...of course. And you came about the coffee shop. You're quite a chip off the old block, you know that? Doing this all *pro bono*, hmm?"

Roger wanted to say yes, but he was too honest.

"My girlfriend works there," he admitted.

"Ah. And is she outside now?"

Faintly, the melody of Peace's tune reached his ears from the street. "I think so. Yes."

"I'd say invite her in, but I don't think my receptionist would like that." He cocked his head, and Roger realised he was being dismissed. The words 'very busy fox' seemed to hang in the air.

"The coffee shop..." he ventured.

"Is safe, my boy."

They shook paws and Roger gathered his papers together. Travelling back down in the elevator, he felt dazed and somewhat anticlimactic. He had been gearing himself up for a tough fight, but Brennan had given in just like that. And how on earth had he known Uncle Bob? They had won, that was the important thing, he told himself.

As he swung through the revolving doors, he gave a thumbs up. Instantly, loud cheers and whoops replaced the singing. An unlikely hero for the masses in his suit and tie, Roger found himself lifted shoulder-high by two bears, one black, one grizzly, and carried through the crowd to where Peace was waiting and waving. His paw was shaken and his tail tweaked as he passed by. He even had flowers thrown at him.

Peace came to meet him on Moon's shoulders. The jackrabbit couldn't reach as high as the bears, but it was high enough for Peace to reach Roger's paw and hold it. He leaned down, she leaned up, and they kissed.

"You did it!" the linsang crowed.

"No, you did it, Peace." Peace, and Uncle Bob. But he wasn't around to thank. "I wasn't getting through to Brennan until the sit-in kicked off."

"It was Frank's idea."

"It was your song."

They smiled at each other, and Roger felt he was on the shoulders of giants figuratively as well as literally.

Then they passed a newsstand, and all the joy left him with a jolt. On the front page of the evening edition, surrounded by weirdoes and freaks of all descriptions, was Peace's photo. Roger's shirt around her shoulders. His arm round her waist.

His face next to hers.

Drop Out

Frank stuck the newspaper photo on the fridge.

Roger took it down.

Frank put up another copy.

Roger gave in.

"If I had the money," Frank said, "I'd buy a print from the newspaper office. Hey, you should do that! It'd be a nice gift for Peace!"

"If you used your talents for something important, instead of constantly refining your technique for bugging me..." Roger raised his paws and dropped the matter.

Nobody at college mentioned the incident. Maybe Roger was unrecognizable under his makeup, or maybe none of them read the local paper.

It was driven out of his mind, temporarily, by the arrival of Wade.

Roger wasn't at all surprised to find a stranger in his living-room. That was one of the joys of sharing with Frank: you also shared with his friends. But the beaver perched on the couch didn't look like someone who'd hang out with Frank. His clothes, blue jeans with a plaid shirt, were positively square, and his hair was clipped close to his head, revealing small, rounded ears.

"Roger! Presenting the answer to our little home improvement conundrum!" Frank pointed at the beaver like a game show hostess displaying the star prize.

"Er, hi." Roger held out a paw. His guest stood and shook it.

"Hi! I'm Wade," the beaver said shyly. His front teeth were prominent, but not cartoonish in the way Roger always imagined beavers, and they didn't seem to constitute a speech impediment.

"Wade here is gonna fix up the bathroom floor, also known as the living-room ceiling," beamed Frank. "Just leave it to Beaver!"

Roger chose to ignore that. "How much will it cost?"

Wade opened his mouth, but Frank shushed him.

"Nada and nix," said the fox. "All my good buddy requires is a place to rack up the Zs for a few days." He rushed on before Roger could translate, and protest. "He can crash in the basement. You won't even know he's there. And nor will anyone else."

No mention of the sit-in. Frank had rushed straight on to his next big idea. Honestly, it was like living with a child.

"We do need that ceiling fixed...You got much stuff?" he asked the beaver.

Wade indicated a knapsack with two patches—a dove and a maple leaf—sewn crookedly on the front pocket.

"Then, welcome, I guess."

It wasn't a huge inconvenience, or a very warm welcome, so he was surprised when Wade's eyes and nose grew moist as he thanked them both.

By the end of the week, as he walked into class unchallenged, Roger was beginning to relax.

"Mind if I sit here?"

"Er, sure. I mean no," Roger replied. "Jane, right?"

"Right!" The chipmunk flipped her tail as she settled into the seat next to him. "And you're Roger." She blinked at him through her spectacles, and smiled.

Roger's mind raced. Girls didn't just sit next to guys, not without a reason, and there was only one reason he knew of. He should tell her he had a girlfriend. But just coming out with that would feel weird, and kind of rude. He tucked his elbows in so he wouldn't accidentally touch the furry arm next to his, and bent his head over his notes.

Jane was short and a little plump, and Roger had always thought she looked fun. When she read her papers out in class, she managed to make the dry legal material interesting and comprehensible, and sometimes even sneaked in a joke or two. He didn't know much about her as a person; he vaguely remembered some team or hobby she was involved in. If he could only remember what it was, he could make some polite reference at the end of the class, show he took an interest before giving her the slip...

"Hey, what's going on out there?"

Brian was staring out the window. On the quad, a group of students sat in a ring. They were too far away for Roger to read the placards they carried, but he could hear a faint sound of chanting.

"Oh, that's a sit-in," he said knowledgeably.

"Who's *that* guy?"

There was only one *that guy* that Roger could see. A red fox in a bright yellow kaftan was always going to stand out in any assembly, except maybe a meeting of the Kaftaned Foxes Association. Even then, Roger thought, Frank would somehow manage to draw attention to himself.

"I have absolutely no idea," he said. He took out his textbook and dropped it hard on his desk.

He wasn't getting off that easy, though. As soon as class ended, Brian bounced up.

"Well, come on! Let's go see what it's all about!"

"Yeah!" Jane flashed Roger a grin. "I *knew* things would get exciting if I stuck with you!"

Roger wondered why on earth anyone would ever think that.

The three law students weren't the first to come and check out the protest. Roger found himself peering around the broad shoulders of some of the jock crowd to get a view. Now he could see that the signs and buttons read "STUDENT POWER", "U.S. OUT", and on Frank's placard, in bold pink: "MAKE LOVE NOT WAR".

"'One, two, three, four, W. D. W. Y. F. W.'" Brian said aloud. "What's that spell?"

"Let's push these hippies off the quad. Hell, right off campus!"

Roger wasn't sure who had spoken, but a chorus of growls and mutters suggested the thought wasn't unique to one individual. A brown bear Roger recognised as the captain of the football team raised his weighty paw.

"Take it easy, fellas..."

A wolf stepped forward, looking as if he might shove the bear aside. "My brother's out in Asia. They're disrespecting him."

"Your brother's out there?" Frank yelled. "Then you should be sitting here with us!"

That did it. The wolf swung round to pinpoint the speaker,

then marched towards Frank with his fists up. "It's you peaceniks who're dragging the war out! We need to be united!"

The crowd was certainly united, and they were no peaceniks. They stormed towards the half-dozen protesters as one, and Brian's ears went flat. Loping ahead—he was a wide receiver, and fast—he placed himself between the two factions, then sat calmly and deliberately down at the edge of the seated ring.

"You a dove, Bry?" asked the wolf.

"Maybe. Not sure. But one thing I'm not is a bully." He smiled as if that settled the matter.

Just then, Roger caught sight of the dean hurrying across the campus towards them. The wolf and the rest of the crowd seemed to remember they had places to be, and slunk away. Brian, now his protection was no longer needed, abandoned his newfound support for the peace movement. He patted Frank's arm, rose, and rejoined Roger.

"Wow, Brian," Roger said. "That was some superhero stuff." He could've stepped up in Frank's defense himself—nobody had to know they were roomies—but he told himself he wouldn't have been as effective as a big, muscular cat. That helped a bit.

"You're not gonna be popular," Jane pointed out.

"No big deal." The puma scratched the fur on his arm and looked away. "Well. Gotta get to practice!" He jogged off in the wake of the rest of the team.

The dean was looking down at Frank, with more bemusement than anger in his expression. "Would you mind telling me what's going on here?" he asked.

Frank didn't mind a bit. He explained in great detail. The dean likely didn't understand all the terminology, but he seemed to get the gist.

"I see," he said. "Well, this behavior does not belong on my quad. Off you go, all of you."

First one protester, then another, slunk away until only Frank remained.

"Very well. You have until noon to remove yourself, Mr Vincent. Otherwise you will be removed from this educational establishment. Permanently."

The dean turned on his hoof and stalked away.

"So," Jane said to Roger. "Want to get a Coke? Not on campus. Out in the real world."

"Sure. Reality sounds pretty good right now."

He paid for the drinks, of course, though Jane offered to go Dutch. The wolverine waitress smiled at them when she brought their RC Cola over, and Roger wanted to blurt that they weren't on a date, but held back.

"Think Frank's gonna give up his sit-in before the dean's deadline?" Jane asked.

"He better," Roger said grimly. "Uh, for his own sake, that is."

"I think he's really brave." Jane took a sip of her drink. "I'm gonna put him in the paper."

That was it—the thing that Roger had forgotten! Jane wrote for the student newspaper! Roger glanced around, feeling trapped in the booth with its red seats. He gripped the edge of the table.

"Speaking of which, I wanted to ask you something." Jane reached in her purse and brought out a folded square of paper. Roger knew before she opened it what it would be. "Is this you?"

Roger looked at the raccoon with the painted face and the arm round his girlfriend. *Was* it him? he wondered. That Roger was far removed from the one who studied law and took girls out for Cokes.

"That's me," he admitted. Jane's eyes lit up behind her glasses.

"It was really great, what you did!" she said. "Can I interview you for the paper?"

"Er, I'd rather you didn't." Roger squirmed.

"C'mon. It would be a real scoop for me. And you'd be a hero."

"I'm not so sure about that."

"Maybe you're right. People are so boring." She sighed. "Is that your girlfriend?"

Roger paused for longer this time, before nodding.

"I thought so! You're so cute together!"

"But you asked me out!" Roger said, unable to stop himself. Jane's eyes, already large by nature and magnified by her glasses, bugged out even more.

"Did you think I was asking you on a date?"

"Yeah. Sorry. That was dumb of me." Fancy flattering himself like that, when all she wanted was a story for her paper! Roger might not have wanted to get involved in an awkward situation, but he realised he'd rather wanted to be wanted. He'd wanted to brag to Peace that a girl had made a move on him but he'd remained faithful. Wow, bad idea.

He felt his face flush under the fur and knew that the insides of his ears would be telltale pink. He stared at Jane, who stared back with an expression of embarrassed horror so identical to Roger's, reflected in her eyes, that he cracked up, and the chipmunk joined in. She laughed until her glasses steamed up, and she took them off to wipe them, her unfocused gaze aimed somewhere behind Roger's left ear.

"You know, I thought college would be different," she said suddenly.

"I'm sorry?"

"Everyone's here to learn, right? You get to think for yourself, you can dress how you like, you don't have to conform, and you'll be respected for being smart, or unique. Not teased."

"Yeah, that's...oh, wait!" Roger smacked himself in the forehead. "No it's not!" Jane didn't laugh, though.

"I was bullied at school," she continued, "and the only reason I don't get bullied at college is I keep my head down and jocks don't bother reading the student paper. I wish I was brave enough to let it all hang out like Frank, not just write about it."

"Well," Roger said. "Frank's a special case."

The chipmunk was bristling and breathing hard. He reached across the table, and when Jane didn't pull away he put his paw on hers and gave it a gentle squeeze. In a sitcom, he thought, Peace would walk into the diner and there'd be a comical misunderstanding before the kiss and make up. But no linsang appeared.

Sitcoms made him think of TV, and that reminded him that his was broken, and that reminded him of Frank. He checked his watch; ten to twelve.

"I need to get back to campus," he said.

"Me too," Jane said immediately, bouncing out of her seat. The cub reporter hot on the trail of her latest story.

"Jane—give me a chance to talk to Frank on my own. Please. I've got to try and fix this before it goes any further. I know it's hot news to you but it's his life on the line."

"Okay, Roger. But you owe me one scoop."

"Of ice cream?" he tried.

"Nope. Of news."

"I'll see what I can do," Roger promised.

Roger nursed the faint hope that Frank would have deserted his post, but the fox was still out on the quad, keeping perfectly still even though a game of softball was now in progress around him. His eyes were closed and Roger could hear him murmuring something under his breath.

None of the players actually touched Frank, but many of them just happened to kick up the dirt as they ran past. As Roger watched, Frank casually flicked his ear at the exact moment the ball passed over it. He could almost believe that the fox was harnessing some kind of trippy hippie power.

Roger knelt down beside him. "Frank. C'mon, Frank. You've made your point. Time to quit while you're ahead."

The dean would reappear at any moment, and Roger would find himself tarnished by association. It could ruin his GPA for good...but he still had a few minutes in which to talk his roomie round. It made economic sense, after all. No college for the fox meant no rent money.

Frank opened one eye a crack.

"Nope," he said.

"Why now?" Roger asked. "Why this?"

"It was you, man. You said I should use my talents for the important things, and I thought: yeah, I oughta."

Roger groaned. "The war's not going to end a single day sooner because you parked your tail on the quad. All that's going to happen is you'll get thrown off your course. You'll have no money and no prospect of getting a job so you can earn some."

"This is about more than bread."

"I know money's not important to you, Frank, but..."

"No, listen. I got a deferral because I applied for college. If I get thrown out, I go to Asia." Frank looked into the distance, his tailtip twitching, as if he was already fighting for his life in the jungles Roger had seen on the news. When Roger had told Jane it was Frank's life on the line, he'd thought he was exaggerating. Apparently not.

"If I protest the war, I might end up getting sent to it. But if I don't protest it, I deserve to go, because I'm not standing up for what I believe in. It's catch-22, man."

"Then write to the paper. Write to your congressman. Write a song. Just don't throw your future away for a dumb sit-in. Please."

Frank lowered his head and rested it on his dangling paws, contemplating his navel. He stayed still for a few moments, then looked up and held out his paw so Roger could help him stand.

"That's not bad for a square, you know."

"Huh?"

"Write to your congressman, write me a song. Write to the paper, cause we gotta right this wrong," sang the fox, and his ears slowly returned to their usual perk. "Needs a little work, of course. Well, guess I'll hit the library." He wandered away.

"Like living with a child," Roger muttered.

As he backed out of range of the softball players Brian trotted up to him, fresh from football practice and a shower. He looked as full of pep as a gum commercial, and his whiskers were perked forward. "So you *do* know that guy!"

"We've...met a couple of times." Roger checked his watch. "I gotta go, man."

He was halfway to his next class before he realised what he'd called his friend.

Between Roger's classes and Peace's shifts, it could be hard to catch a conversation with his girlfriend, but this afternoon he badly wanted to. He found her in the kitchen of the coffee shop, washing plates. Marge, the badger who ran the place and who couldn't do enough for Roger since his stand-off with the property developer, snatched the dishcloth from Peace's paw and practically shooed them both up to the linsang's little bedroom.

In the evening, with the candles lit, it was cosy. Now, with the sun over the other side of the building, the room seemed bleak and cold despite the Indian scarves pinned to the wall, and the posters of musicians Roger didn't recognize.

"Would you rather go for a walk?" he offered.

"No, I'm good. Pretty tired." Peace yawned, showing off her perfect, pointed teeth and the pink curl of her tongue, and flowed into Roger's lap. She fit so well, her tail around his hip and her head under his chin, that it hardly mattered when Roger's feet went to sleep, followed by his legs. He just sat and stroked her ears, marvelling, as usual, at how light and thin she was under her golden fur. With her paws tucked under her body, against his chest, she looked like a spotted snake. Her shoulder twitched, and Roger reached down her shirt to scratch it for her. She wasn't wearing a bra.

"Mm. Carry on round, if you like."

"I'll stretch the neck of your shirt."

"It's only a material possession."

Roger snorted at the pun and slid his paw around her ribs to the front. There he paused; there were two—well, three—areas of Peace that he had always considered off limits. Hesitantly, he stroked, then pressed with a finger, then cupped in his palm.

"So, how was college?"

"Peace, I can either tell you about my day or make out with you. I don't think I can manage both at once."

"Okay, then." She rolled over and pushed herself into a sitting position by bracing her back against Roger's chest and wriggling. Her head tilted back so it rested on his shoulder.

"Leave your paw where it is," she instructed, upside-down, "and tell me about your day."

Roger kissed her nose. Then he filled her in on Frank's one-fox protest movement and its end.

"Poor Frank. I hope he made people think, at least."

Maybe think about what a nuisance he was. Roger didn't say that, though. "He made Brian think. And Jane wanted to put him in the campus paper."

"I didn't know you had a friend called Jane."

That was because, up till now, he hadn't. "She's in my class."

"She must be smart," Peace said, sounding as if it bothered her.

The best reassurance he could think of was to kiss her, so he did. Peace grabbed him round the neck, and suddenly Roger was on his back, on the floor, with Peace on top of him. Her tail beat against his legs and her whiskers tickled his face. He held one paw to the back of her head, keeping her slender muzzle within reach so he could go on kissing it. When Peace's alarm clock suddenly rang, they snapped apart.

"Oh, I have to do my set soon," Peace groaned, sitting up. She bounced on Roger's stomach a couple of times.

"Ow! Stop!" With a mighty effort, Roger grabbed the linsang's wrists and wrestled her off as she giggled and struggled. His paws on hers, he laid her on her back and held her there.

"No," Peace said, and he let go at once. "Don't pin me down. I don't like it."

Roger knew that, of course, though he hadn't realized Peace's need for freedom was so literal. He knelt on the floor and watched as she picked herself up, still breathless from giggling, her eyes very bright. She ran a brush through her long hair, pulled her T-shirt straight, then turned her attention to her tail, flexing round so she could hold it. There was a tangle near the base, and she winced as she tried to comb it out with her claws.

"Roger?"

"Sure." He draped her tail around his shoulders and brushed

at the matted area with firm, gentle strokes until the knot of hairs parted.

"I'll be late," Peace said, flicking her tail. Newly brushed, her fur gleamed. A few loose hairs landed on Roger's arms and shirt, marking him with her scent and speckling him with gold.

"I love you," he said.

He'd wanted to say it for a long time, but he had been half-afraid of what Peace's reaction might be. For all he knew she'd interpret it as an attempt to trap her, classify her, own her. Peace talked a lot about love for all, and free love, but she'd never talked about a more specific, personal kind. If she didn't feel the way he did, it would be embarrassing at best, at worst the end of whatever they had. But now the words came out before he could stop them.

Roger needn't have worried. Peace's golden face seemed to glow, and she twisted round to face him, giving her toothy, kooky grin.

"I love you too," she whispered. "Now get out of here! I need to warm up my vocal cords."

"I'll warm them up for you," Roger offered, giddy with triumph. Peace swatted him out with her tail, and he bounced home as if he was walking on air. He felt as though he could even have walked across his own bathroom floor.

When Roger came home the next evening, he was greeted by the sound of cheerful whistling. The floor and furniture in the living-room were shrouded in sheets. The smell of Frank's home-rolled cigarettes mingled with the sweetness of sawdust and the sharp tang of fresh paint. Wade was up a ladder, adding a coat of plaster to a ceiling already smooth and gleaming white. He reached down to replenish his brush from a bucket held by

Frank. The fox's head and shoulders were liberally splashed with drips.

"You look like one of the statues in Central Park," Roger told him. Frank jumped.

"Oh, hi! We were hoping to have this done by the time you got in."

"Never mind—you've done a great job. Where'd you get the plaster...and the wood...and the tools?"

"Weird's garage," Frank said proudly, "and the junkyard. You've got a floor made of doors, man, how freaky is that?"

"Just so long as you don't, er..." Wade frowned, as if trying to think of something, "*break on through to the other side!*"

From the delighted grin he exchanged with Frank, Roger assumed this was a joke.

"Did you want me to paint the walls, too?" the beaver asked.

"Oh, that would be..."

"We thought we could do a mural," added Frank.

"No, thanks, just the ceiling will be fine. Now, if you don't mind, I'm going to head to bed."

"If you need to use the bathroom, just stay near the walls for now!" Wade called after him.

"Yeah, man! Live life on the edge! Explore the outer limits! The center cannot hold!"

"Good *night*, Frank."

The Fuzz

Roger walked smiling down Bleecker Street. It was Sunday morning, it was sunny, and he was seeing Peace later. His roommate had gone out the night before and the raccoon had spent a blissful evening on his own, watching the replacement TV Frank had wheedled out of Weird, under a whole and perfect ceiling. When the otter lady approached him outside the liquor store, he sang out a happy *Good morning!* and walked on by.

A month ago he wouldn't have dared walk these streets, even if he'd wanted to. They were populated by all the Frank types in New York, and Roger got enough of that at home. Strange clothes, strange smells, strange music—it all either bugged him or plain scared him. Now, even the wino sitting on the curb didn't faze him. Roger nodded, and the old guy raised his brown-paper-bag-wrapped bottle to him.

He stared at the hand-written sign in the window of a store selling health food. 'FRESH FLAKES', it promised. Yeah, you got that right, thought Roger.

Why was he here at all? He wanted to get Peace a present.

He'd visited Macy's and spent hours going from floor to floor, but nothing seemed right for his beautiful linsang. Everything was mass-produced, soulless—he knew she'd hate it all.

The sparkle of jewellery in a window display grabbed his attention. There were necklaces and pendants: strings of colored beads, or symbols on leather thongs. Somewhere in there, he knew, was the perfect gift for Peace.

The interior of the shop was dark. A bulb dangled on a cord, but it didn't so much give light as make the colors of the goods glow.

A tabby cat and a rough, shaggy dog watched Roger from behind the counter. The cat was wearing Day-Glo paint on her face, and it shone under the weird light.

"Squaresville," said the dog, obviously intending Roger to hear.

"Jay! Don't be so judgmental," tutted the tabby. "Can I help you?"

"Could I look at the bracelets in the window?" asked Roger.

"Sure! I make those myself." The tabby walked over to the window, trailing her red skirt and a scent Roger recognized, these days, as patchouli. She pulled out the tray of jewellery and put it on the counter in front of Roger.

He took a long time to make up his mind, lifting out the beads and semiprecious stones and holding them up to the light. The gems had meanings, he knew, but he wasn't sure what any of them were; he'd hate to give her the wrong thing. A peace symbol for Peace? Too corny?

At last he picked a circle of star-shaped glass beads in all the colors of the rainbow.

"You're a little out of your territory, aren't you?" said the tabby, not unkindly. "Is this for someone special?"

"Do you know a girl called Peace Man?" Roger asked.

"No, but she sounds a gas!"

"Is that good? Because if so, yes. She's a gas." Roger returned the tabby's smile and walked out into the sunshine, his gift in his pocket.

His eyes were still adjusting after the dark cavern of the shop when paws grabbed him round the waist. Roger struggled and shrieked. He was being mugged! They would take everything, beat him up, tear his clothes. Why had he come to this neighborhood? He should have listened to his mother's warnings!

He was scooped off his feet and pressed against a wall, the rough bricks grazing his muzzle. Blinking through tears, Roger looked down at the paws that held him.

He saw the shaggy gray coat of a wolfhound, and the dark, buttoned sleeve of a police dog.

"Paws against the wall and spread your legs. No funny stuff," snarled the cop.

Roger obeyed. He turned his head to one side, leaning against the wall, and noticed how the passers-by pretended not to see them. So this was what 'don't mess with someone else's scene' really meant: don't help someone in trouble!

He had always respected the police, as his mother had taught him, and shaken his head when Frank and his friends complained about 'the fuzz'. Even when they'd broken up the sit-in, Roger had felt in more danger from his fellow protesters than from the cops. If you'd done nothing wrong you had nothing to fear from the law. To be treated this way by the people he'd always considered friends and protectors was terrifying.

From the corner of his eye, he saw a second dog step forward —a setter. Auburn paws turned his pockets inside out, scattering wallet, handkerchief, keys, pencils and a precious photograph of Peace. His clothes were shaken out, yanking his shirt from his pants. Then the dog's cold nose went to his neck.

He stifled a yelp as the setter sniffed him carefully from head to foot, patting his ribs and pant legs as he went.

"Clean," said the sniffer dog to his partner, straightening up. "But I can smell it all over him. You were lucky this time, buddy." He picked Roger up by his elbows, swung him round, and dusted him down. Then he pretended to stumble, and jabbed the raccoon hard in the stomach. "Oops! Have a nice day!"

As the two dogs sauntered off Roger doubled over on the curb, his ears roaring and his eyes full of television interference. A paw rested on his shoulder—a gentle touch, this time.

"Those brutes!" It was the tabby from the shop. "I'm so sorry I couldn't help—if I make any more trouble they'll close me down. Let me get you a cup of herbal tea."

"No...thanks," puffed Roger. "Just want to go home." He let her help him up. "What...they looking for?"

Her mouth twitched in a quick smile among the concern. "Dope," she told him. "Drugs! Like anyone couldn't tell you were clean just by looking at you. You poor kid!"

She helped him gather up his possessions, and Roger tottered away.

The streets of the Village no longer seemed friendly. The old wino reached out a paw as he passed, calling "Bobby? Bobby!" and Roger crossed the street, head down. The people walking past in their Technicolor clothes and American flags, they all ignored him. He wasn't one of them, but he'd been tarred with the same brush. Drugs! Him! And he knew full well why he smelled of the stuff. Frank and his dumb friends! Just wait till he got home! Even if Frank was still in bed, Roger was gonna drag him out by the scruff of his neck and have this out with him.

These thoughts occupied him all the way home. From the end of the street, he spotted a small figure squatting on the doorstep and quickened his pace.

For the first time since their first meeting, he wasn't pleased to see Peace Man. He was already shouting when he arrived, yelling about *your friends* and *my roomie* and *had enough*, but he stopped in mid-flow when he saw that Peace was crying.

"What is it? Darling, what's wrong?" he asked, wrapping his black paws around her neck and nuzzling her tearstained cheeks. She was sobbing too hard to speak at first; she just clutched his paw tight and shook her head. After a few minutes she managed to choke out:

"They've arrested Frank!"

"Good!" Roger snapped, scowling under his black mask. Peace cringed away as though he'd hit her, but he was too angry to stop. "I've just been beaten up by two cops because they could smell drugs on me! Frank's got drugs in my home, I know it! Oh God, did they search the house? Did they find anything?"

"Roger, stop, please." The linsang struck feebly at him without looking, punching him in the thigh. "They didn't arrest him for drugs, they arrested him because he's gay."

Roger felt a lump rise in his throat. His girlfriend was angry with him, his roommate was under arrest...and Peace hadn't even reacted when he told her about his encounter with the law. He was still shocked and scared, his knees hurt where he'd hit the pavement earlier, and he wanted to curl up and cry.

Peace was hunched on the step, tears on her cheeks, looking up at Roger with a hopeful, confident expression—like a child who knows that Mom or Dad will fix the scraped elbow or the broken toy.

"You can get him out, can't you?" she said. "You're a lawyer!"

"I'm not a lawyer yet," said Roger, but he stood up straighter and brushed the dust off his clothes. He'd fix this for her, earn her thanks and admiration. Consideration for Frank came a guilty second.

"Let's sit down and have a coffee first," he said. "Think this thing through."

While Roger put the coffee on and selected a tie, Peace couldn't stop talking. "They came to the coffee shop—burst in, he was just sitting talking to me. He put up a fight because he thought they were after Wade, then they started calling him names and we realised what it was about. We tried to find Davy and warn him but no one's seen him, I hope he's safe. They beat you up? What happened? Are you okay?"

"I'm fine," Roger told her, putting their mugs down and sitting beside her on Frank's beanbag. She moved behind him and began to massage his shoulders. As her slim, guitar player's fingers kneaded, she pressed her knees to his sides and kissed his head and neck.

Wait a second, Roger thought. Why would the cops be after *Wade*?

The phone made them both jump. Roger picked it up on the second ring.

"Hey man, it's me." Frank sounded tired and frightened. "This is, like, my one phone call."

"Don't worry, Frank, we're coming."

They drove to the police station in Roger's Plymouth, neither of them saying much.

"Do you want to stay here?" Roger asked when they arrived. He rubbed his black paws together nervously.

"No, I want to see Frank—and be with you," Peace replied. Roger wasn't sure she'd help his attempt to look like a lawyer, dressed as she was in cut-off, faded jeans and a kid's T-shirt, but he was flattered nonetheless.

The ram on the desk looked them up and down. "No visitors," he said. "This ain't a hotel."

Twenty-four hours previously, Roger would have accepted that the police, the guardians of the law, were always in the right. Now he'd seen how wrong they could be, he wasn't giving up that easily. "I'm his lawyer."

"You? You're a kid." The sergeant lowered his hard poll and turned his attention back to his comic book.

"Do you have a bathroom?" Peace asked.

"Not for public use," the ram replied without looking up.

Peace retched, clapping one hand to her mouth and the other to her stomach. "Please!" she gasped. Faced with the prospect of mopping the floor, the ram leaped up and unlocked the heavy door beside the desk.

"Second on the right!" he called as Peace grabbed Roger by the paw and ran.

To the raccoon's surprise, she didn't rush into the bathroom. Instead, she turned her back to Roger and twisted her paws up between her shoulders. "Pretend you're arresting me!"

"What?"

"You're in a suit, I'm a dirty hippie." She waved her clasped paws at him. Remembering her dislike of being pinned, Roger took her wrists gingerly.

"Harder." He increased his grip and lifted his paws an inch or two so Peace looked genuinely uncomfortable.

A sign on the wall directed them to CELLS. They passed a cleaner and a hurrying, uniformed officer, neither of whom spared them a glance.

"This is kind of a turn-on," Peace whispered.

"Shut up!" Roger hissed. Then he said it louder and jerked her wrists for the benefit of a fat ginger cat strolling by with a box of donuts. Now that Peace mentioned it, it was kind of a turn-on...

Roger stopped dead, making Peace stumble backwards. He released her and made room at the small window in the office door.

Peace gasped. "That sneaky..."

Sitting in the office, leaning back and looking pleased with himself, was Davy. An almost unrecognizable Davy, long fur brushed out of his eyes, clad in a dark gray suit with a chalk pinstripe.

Before Roger could begin to think of a plan, Peace Man had burst into the office. Once in, her voice deserted her and she could only stand in front of Davy's desk, pointing a finger at him as her huge tail lashed behind her.

"Entrapment," said Roger, stepping into the breach, "is a very serious thing, Davy, if that's really your name."

The big sheepdog looked from one to the other. "Only if there was no original intent to commit a crime. And in your friend's case, I'd say there was." He cracked his knuckles. When he stood up, he towered above them both. "I don't know how you got in here, but..."

"Do you want us to leave, Davy-dog?" Peace asked. "Because we'll go straight to the press."

"The press won't give a damn. Nor will the Mayor. Don't worry, you'll get your boyfriend back." He looked from one to the other, addressing them both. "He might not be quite the same shape as before, mind. Some of my colleagues have strong feelings about his kind."

"The Village Voice will care."

"So will the student paper," Roger added, thinking of Jane.

"You could have a riot on your paws," said the linsang, warming to her theme. "Would you like that?"

"A chance to beat up a pack of hippies and fruits? I'd love it."

"Do your colleagues know you've been working on this little

undercover deception?" Roger asked. "Or was it for extra credit?"

"Or do you just enjoy hanging out in gay clubs?"

Davy raised a paw, and Roger realized that if he laid so much as a single pad on Peace, Roger would be morally obliged to kill him.

Peace skipped out of reach. "I think you liked it, Davy!" she called. "In fact, I'm pretty sure..." She fished in the pockets of her jeans and produced a crumpled photo. Roger only caught a glimpse as she fluttered it in front of the sheepdog's nose, but he made out Frank and Davy. In the coffee shop. Kissing.

"You look so cute together!" Peace beamed.

Davy's eyes were panicked. It was one thing to trick Frank, leading him on and getting his guard down until he gave himself away, but appearing in a photograph with his tongue down the fox's throat was going to be a lot harder to explain.

"Give me that!"

"Not until you give us Frank!"

Davy moved towards her, but Roger put a paw on his shoulder. "I won't let you touch her," he promised, "and if you call for help, whoever you call gets to see the picture. Now, why don't you take us to the cells like a good doggy?" Where had that come from? Frank would have accused him of going on a 'crazy power trip'. Well, this trip would benefit Frank.

Frank looked very small in the cell, curled up with his arms around his knees and his ears pressed against his skull. His face lit up when he saw Roger and Peace, but when Davy appeared behind them, smartly dressed and holding a ring of keys, the fox's expression changed to absolute shock and horror. It should have been comical, but even Roger couldn't laugh at him.

Davy avoided Frank's eyes as he unlocked the door. As Frank stepped through, the sheepdog held out his paw for the photo, which he ripped into quarters and stuffed in his pocket.

"Thanks, Peace. Rodge." And that was all Frank said, all the way home.

Apparently news travelled fast on the coffee shop grapevine. Moon the jackrabbit was waiting outside Roger's brownstone.

She hugged Peace and kissed her—on the lips, Roger noticed —before turning to Roger, who stepped back hastily.

"Well done," Moon beamed. She made no attempt to touch him, after all, and Roger suddenly felt sorry that he had established himself as too square for hugs. He busied himself unlocking the door.

Frank stood in the doorway of his home, looking around as if not only the house but the entire planet was new to him. Moon took his arm and led him into the living-room, raising her eyebrows at Peace and Roger over her shoulder.

"Will he be okay?" Roger whispered.

"With Moon around, as okay as he can be. Let's go upstairs."

They sat on Roger's bed, holding paws and trying not to tune in to the muffled voices downstairs. Peace was shivering in her T-shirt, so Roger wrapped the bedspread around her. She snuggled down against the pillow and patted the sheet, inviting Roger in with her. He slipped off his suit jacket, kicked his shoes under the bed and held the linsang against his chest, trying to warm her with his body. He could feel her breathing.

"Your sheets smell of you," she said.

"Peace. Why did you have that photo in your pocket? Of Frank and Davy?"

Peace looked down at her toes, wriggling under the bedspread. "I...I just thought they were so sweet together. I guess I hoped I'd find something like that one day myself. But it was all fake."

Roger squeezed her shoulder. "It wasn't fake for Frank. And it's not fake for me."

"When Davy tipped Frank off about the police at the sit-in.

Do you think it was because he really cared about him? Or because it might have blown his cover?"

"Who knows? He sure spent a long time on Frank, when one kiss would have been more than enough to arrest him. Maybe he really did have feelings for him, but his colleagues found out and he had to save himself. You want to go back to the police station and ask?"

"No." She slipped her fingers inside the waistband of his shorts. Roger gasped, and not just because her paws were cold.

"I liked it when you pretended to be a cop. Do it again!" Her smile was all teeth.

"Miss Man, you're under arrest for...for being too far out!" Roger improvised. "Your grooviness violates several state laws. Ma'am, I'm afraid I'm gonna have to ask you to sleep with me."

She cocked her head. Roger realized what he'd said, and nodded. Giggling, they grabbed at each other's clothes. Peace crumpled Roger's shirt and suit pants into a ball and threw them into the corner. Roger, even in the heat of the moment, folded Peace's rainbow T-shirt neatly in four and dropped it beside the bed.

The doorbell rang.

"Leave it," Peace moaned, snatching at Roger's tail as he hopped out of bed.

"Can't. Might be my mom!" He peered cautiously out the bedroom window at the figure on the doorstep.

It was Brian, his puma classmate.

Flower Power

"Leave it," Peace said again, sitting up in bed with that amazing tail draped round her shoulders so it hung between her breasts.

"It could be important. I'll get rid of him," Roger muttered, struggling into his shirt as Brian, on the doorstep, pressed the bell again.

The truth was that Roger didn't want his clean-cut puma friend to see Frank, or any of Frank's weird buddies. Or Peace? he asked himself as he pattered down the stairs. No—he wanted to introduce his girlfriend to Brian, very much. Only not now this minute.

There was no sound from the living-room; Frank must still be in there with Moon. Grateful for this small mercy, Roger opened the door.

"Hi!" Glossy and smartly-suited, the puma bounced up the steps and into the hall. "You must be studying too hard—you've got dark circles under your eyes!"

The raccoon laughed politely at the old joke. "What's up, Bry?"

"Do you have a copy of *Law in Feral Societies*? I need it for my assignment and all the library copies are out."

"Sure—I've got one in my room. Wait here."

"No problem, I'll come up," Brian said at once. He'd visited a couple of times before Roger decided that Frank had rendered his house off-limits to respectable college students. Roger's bedroom had, up till now, remained a bastion of decency, but it was definitely off-limits today. His tail bushing with panic, he dashed around Brian and blocked his access to the stairs.

Brian laughed, puzzled, and dodged left in one smooth, feline movement that left Roger off-balance. Never try to block a footballer, the raccoon told himself as he grabbed the banister. Brian was already loping up the stairs, but he stopped when Peace Man appeared at the top.

The puma's eyes went huge and his jaw actually dropped. Roger didn't know whether to be proud or cross that his girlfriend had inspired such a reaction, so he kept quiet.

"You must be Brian," Peace said. She was wearing Roger's suit jacket over her bare chest. "Roger's told me so much about you."

"And you're Peace," Brian replied, taking the stairs two at a time to hold her paw and shake it. "Wow! I've never met a linsang before. You've made Roger very happy, you know."

Over the puma's head, Peace's eyes met Roger's. He nodded. She blushed.

"Brian, want a coffee?" She took his paw in that casual way she had. Needles of jealousy prickled over Roger's skin, while Brian's ears blushed pink. The three of them headed into the kitchen, where Peace operated Roger's black and chrome coffee machine like a pinball wizard. Brian, who had always struck Roger as the quiet type, couldn't stop talking, questioning Peace:

"Are you a hippie?"

"I believe in peace. And I like good music. So, I guess!"

"Do you take drugs?"

"I used to, but I haven't since I met Roger."

"What's it like?"

"It takes you away from reality for a while. But lately, reality hasn't been such a bad gig."

Roger stirred his coffee fiercely. He'd never asked the drug question, and he was a little shocked by both Brian and Peace. Now she was telling him about their morning, and before he could stop her it had all come out: impersonating a police officer, threatening and blackmailing a detective. Brian's expression was horrified, and Roger braced himself for a lecture on his reckless behavior.

"I can't believe he was stringing Frank along all that time! What a sleazeball!" the puma declared, his eyes round as moons.

Just then, Frank dragged himself into the kitchen. Brian, appalled, clapped his paws over his mouth. Frank gave a small smile.

"You're a friend of Roger's, I can tell by the suit. Is that fresh coffee I smell?"

He turned his back to them and busied himself with the coffee pot.

"I remember you from the sit-in on campus," Brian said timidly. "I like your...dress?"

"It's a kaftan, man," Frank said automatically.

"You must think I'm pretty square, huh?" Brian was trying to be *hip*, now? Roger cringed silently, but Frank, mug in paw, gave the puma another smile—a proper one.

"Not at all. I think you look like a real cool cat! Any friend of my roomie's is a friend of mine—c'mon into the living-room."

"Brian was just leaving. He's got a paper to write," Roger said quickly.

"Oh, no, I can stay for a while! Thanks."

Could Roger's day get any more surreal? Maybe he was the

one on drugs. He'd been assaulted by the police, he'd committed a daring rescue, and now his college friend was sitting on his living-room floor while Moon taught him yoga positions.

"This one's very relaxing, Roger—you should try it. You're tense," the jackrabbit told him.

"Feels good," Brian agreed, stretching until his spine clicked.

"Making people relax is my specialty," Moon told him. "I'm a receptionist at a dentist's office."

"Really?" Roger tried to imagine her in a crisp uniform instead of her flowing velvet dress.

"That's how I met Frank. He came in for a filling and said he hoped we had some good drugs."

"And you said you had something better," Frank chimed in, "and you gave me my mantra."

"And what was your mantra?" Moon asked, kneading Roger's shoulders.

"*I am a rock,*" intoned Frank reverently. "I said that in my head the whole way through and I didn't feel a thing. I had gas too, of course," he added.

Peace moved towards Roger on the couch and laid her head on his lap while she rested her feet on the arm. No feet on the furniture was one of Roger's rules, but he didn't want to scold her in front of everyone. Besides, she felt so warm and right with her shoulder snuggled up to his knee, he couldn't even feel embarrassed at this display of affection in front of Brian.

The puma was chatting quietly with Frank. Roger tuned himself out of their conversation and stroked the soft fur behind Peace's ears to make her smile. He touched his fingers to her face so each one rested on a spot, and rubbed her cheek with his thumb. She hunched her shoulders, giggling sleepily. "Tickles," she murmured.

Watching her whiskers tremble as she breathed was as

hypnotic as gazing into Frank's lava lamp. When Brian got to his feet, Peace and Roger both jumped.

"I really had better go write that paper," the puma said sadly. "Can I visit again soon?"

"Sure, Bry. See you in class tomorrow," Roger replied. "I would see you out, but..."

Peace, though, was already stretching and swinging her legs off the couch. "I better go too. Rehearsal. Are you coming tonight, Roger? How about you, Brian?"

Brian looked at Roger as though asking permission. "I have to work," the raccoon groaned, "but you go, Brian. You know where the coffee shop is, right?"

"Right. See you tomorrow! Peace, nice to meet you, see you tonight!"

When Brian and Roger met the next day, each with a paper to turn in, Brian couldn't stop talking about the linsang.

"What a voice! She's really talented. On her break she told me about that song she wrote, Song for Joe, and...but you know all that."

"Mm." Roger nodded. Talking about Peace while on campus still made him feel uneasy. It wasn't that he was ashamed of her, exactly—it just felt out of place in this austere, academic environment. No wonder she'd dropped out.

From then on, though, he had plenty of opportunities to talk to Brian outside of college. The puma dropped in several times a week to hang out with Roger, Peace and especially Frank, with whom he seemed to click straight away. Roger had never sought Frank's friendship, but he resented how easily Brian had won it.

Peace's, too—she made friends easily, of course she did, everyone loved her. There was nothing in the way she grabbed at Brian's tail in passing, or the way he used it to swat her legs. Roger had to tell himself that, or go mad. But he couldn't help noticing that Peace and Brian often split off from the rest of the group to talk quietly in a corner, heads together. If Roger approached, they welcomed him with smiles but always started a new topic of conversation and refused to tell him the old one.

"Your GPA is slipping, Mr Jones. If you're going to pass the LSAT, you need to buckle down PDQ." The bobcat raised one furry eyebrow and glared at Roger. "That was a joke. So was your last assignment."

"Yes, sir."

"I didn't fight in Europe so lazy bums like you could abuse their freedom by sleeping through my classes."

"No, sir."

"Nor did I fight so I could see it all happen again in my lifetime," he continued in a gentler voice. "But that is my personal opinion and I keep it off campus. That's all, Mr Jones."

"Thank you, sir."

Brian was waiting outside the classroom.

"He give you a hard time?"

"Yeah. I deserve it, though. Need to get some serious studying done."

"Shall I come round tonight? We can get Chinese, study together. Jane, too. She really wants to meet Frank and everyone."

So Brian had been shooting his muzzle off to Jane, had he? Roger wasn't sure he needed anyone else from college joining his living-room menagerie, but it would have seemed rude to refuse. They reached Roger's place loaded down with cardboard cartons.

"Why'd you order so much extra?" Jane asked.

"You'll see."

"Hi, squares," leered Weird as Roger led his friends in.

"Ignore my boorish companion, puma pal and damsel whose name I do not yet know! Do I smell the rarest spices of the mysterious Orient?"

"Yes, Frank, and I brought enough for you. And you, Weird." Roger rolled his eyes.

"Thanks, man!" Frank pounced, then paused. "Oh, hey. How about Wade?"

"I've barely seen him since he finished fixing the floor. He hasn't died down there, has he?"

"No, man, he just didn't want to bug you. Wade!" Frank hollered. "Chuck wagon's here!"

"I don't suppose you know how long he's planning to stay?" Roger whispered it quickly, before Wade could arrive and get upset.

"Just till he can get his ride to Canada. Shouldn't be long. Hey, Weird, don't bogart the spring rolls."

Frank's idea of time tended to be elastic, but Roger didn't push him. He assumed, takeouts aside, that Frank was feeding his Canadian friend, since no more of Roger's food was disappearing than it usually did—though the coffee tin was running low. And, really, a lot of the time, he forgot Wade was there.

Now the beaver waddled up from the basement, lured by the siren call of takeout. At Roger's invitation, he dug gratefully in to the chow mein. Everyone was digging in—except the linsang.

"Peace? You in?"

Doubtfully, Peace accepted a pair of chopsticks in their paper sheath and lifted a piece of sweet and sour chicken to her mouth. She pulled a face.

"Don't you like it?" Roger was hurt in his primal hunter-gatherer sensibilities.

"Roger, I'm Chinese," she said when she'd swallowed. "If

you ate mac and cheese in China, you might find it wasn't quite like your mom's, either."

"I forgot. Sorry."

Weird laughed out loud; Frank chuckled; Brian and Jane smiled shyly at the linsang. Roger felt his face and ears burning, and it had nothing to do with the hot sauce on his prawn balls.

"Everyone, this is Jane," he said, to cover his confusion. The chipmunk waved and sat down next to Peace, watching as she tuned Frank's guitar.

Frank upended the last carton of egg fried rice above his muzzle and licked out the corners.

"Who wants ice cream?" he demanded.

"Frank!" groaned Roger, standing up with one paw over his belly. "Don't mention food to me for at least eight hours! Besides, we have to study."

Brian looked a little wistfully at Frank. Surely he couldn't be hungry still? Roger nudged him.

"Oh! Oh, yeah."

Peace got up to follow them, holding her guitar.

"I really do need to work, Peace," Roger said reluctantly. "That's my scene. Tonight, at least."

The linsang's tail flopped to the floor, and Roger felt horrible. They were both free to do their own thing, Peace had told him so often enough, but once again he was rubbing her nose in the fact that he was doing a college degree and she wasn't. Of course he'd rather Peace was with him! But he was flunking out! He'd make it up to her later.

"I hope I can hear you sing some time," Jane said as she stood up. "Brian's told me you're good."

"Let the kids do their homework," said Weird. He patted his lap. "Come and have a massage."

"Not from *you*," Peace said. She stuck her tongue out at him and sat by Frank, who laid his paw protectively on the base of her tail.

Reasonably satisfied with the state of affairs in his living-room, Roger took Brian and Jane upstairs.

The evening Roger returned home late following a flat tire and a long walk in the rain to the nearest garage, he found that Brian had dropped round and been admitted to the living-room, in Roger's absence, by Frank. The gang was all here: Peace, Moon, Weird the coyote, Anna and Tom the cat couple. The air was heavy with incense and something else.

"Are you smoking?"

"Only cloves, man," Frank said, waving a black cigarette at him.

"You're not supposed to be smoking anything in here! This is my mom's couch...my mom's carpet."

Brian was hiding one paw behind his back, his ears folded in a demure expression of mute apology.

"Brian! Not you too!"

The guilty parties stubbed out their cigarettes in a saucer—all except Weird, who blew a cloud of scented smoke in Roger's face and held the butt an inch from the carpet, smirking, before flicking it out of the open window to the street below. The coyote, with his odd, milky eyes, still frightened Roger, but he didn't dare ask him to go. What if he refused? Roger just had to trust Frank to keep him under control, and he wouldn't have trusted Frank with a sea-monkey.

"Did you like that, before Mr Establishment here made you stub it out?" Weird asked Brian. The puma looked awkwardly from the coyote to Roger.

"It was kinda like cough medicine," he said at last, rubbing his paw under his chin.

"Cough medicine! Now there's a trip!" Frank exclaimed. "You ever get a cough medicine high, Brian?"

"No..." the puma admitted, "but I did hallucinate once with the flu."

The sight of Brian's round, happy face as he gazed at Frank was driving Roger nuts. His paws curled into fists, the claws hurting his pads.

"Can't you see they're making fun of you?" he shouted. He stormed out, slamming the door, but he could still hear the laughter behind him, with Weird cackling loudest and longest.

At least Peace hadn't joined in—or not audibly. After a couple of minutes he heard soft footsteps, and she followed him into the kitchen. He turned, expecting the comfort of a hug.

"That was rude, Roger. Rude to Frank, and rude to Brian." She crossed her arms.

This was not the reaction Roger needed. Couldn't she see he was upset?

"I'm just sick of this...this double life. I'm failing at college because I got caught up in Frank's dropout lifestyle and, like a fool, I've been trying to help. Meanwhile you're all laughing at me—you, and Frank, and Weird, even Bry. Poor, square Roger, he just doesn't dig our scene, man."

"Is that really what you think?" Peace asked, in a small, cold voice Roger had never heard her use before. Her teeth were bared. Even now, he couldn't help noticing how adorably tiny they were. "I thought you were beginning to understand, but you still have a down on Frank. I know he's kind of intense, but he's my friend."

As if he was standing on the bathroom floor before Wade's fix, Roger felt the ground beneath him crumble, and tried to backpedal.

"It's not you—I didn't mean—it's all so hard for me..."

"It hasn't been easy for me either, Roger, watching you look over your shoulder all the time in case someone's judging you for going out with me. I remember your face the first time Brian showed up—you were terrified of him seeing you with me. But he's such a sweetheart, of course it didn't matter to him."

"Oh, *Brian*! I'm glad you think he's a sweetheart. After all, you've been spending a lot of time together." Roger bristled. "Or did you think I wouldn't notice?"

"Maybe I thought you might loosen up."

Loosen up? It was one of Frank's favorite phrases, and it drove Roger up the wall. Loosen up about me eating your food. Loosen up about the rent.

Roger, he informed Peace in a voice that was barely under a yell, had been jumped by cops while he was minding his own business, he had deceived officers of the law to get Frank out of jail, and this was the thanks he got back. And all golden boy Brian had to do was show up and he was suddenly everyone's best buddy!

Roger couldn't think where all this was coming from, but now he'd started he couldn't stop flapping his muzzle. His jealousy, his insecurity, his uptightness, his grade worries and the overwhelming feeling that he simply didn't belong in Peace and Frank's world, all swirled and spread in the air around him like tie-dye. Moon would have said his aura was bad. He felt as if his everything was bad.

"You like Brian so much, you can keep him. With my blessing," he finished up.

Peace listened, her dark eyes fixed on his face. Gradually, her tail lowered until it dragged in the dust and crumbs on the kitchen floor (Frank evidently felt the bathroom repairs had written off his housekeeping debt).

"Peace?" Roger was scared now. She must know he hadn't meant any of that. "Say something."

"I just don't think this love thing is meant to be such hard work." She marched towards the door, turning back to face him with her paw on the handle. "By the way, you don't need to worry about Brian. Apart from anything else, he's not the type to cheat on a friend."

Roger watched her tail swish out of sight and heard the latch of the front door click behind her. The sound was like a book closing on the last page. He rammed his paws in his pockets and found a small, lumpy object. The bracelet—the rainbow stars he'd bought Peace in the Village, the Sunday morning of Frank's arrest. He'd been waiting for the right time to give it to her.

It looked like he'd left it too late.

Go Now

Roger held on to the counter for a second, letting the shock of it all wash over him. Then he sprinted for the front door, hoping to catch Peace before she vanished from sight around the corner.

He didn't make it. Halfway across the hall, Frank—slow-moving, chilled-out Frank who had never, to Roger's knowledge, participated in a competitive sport in his life—tackled the raccoon to the floor.

"Let her go, man! Just let her go!" Frank yelled in Roger's ear. Roger, knees and elbows smarting, struggled free and got to his feet with as much dignity as he could manage. Frank was staring at him bug-eyed, whether from anger, surprise or the effort of physical exertion Roger couldn't tell.

The raccoon dusted himself off and nodded curtly to his roommate. Without a word, he dragged himself up the stairs, closed his bedroom door behind him and collapsed on the bed.

The sheets still smelled of her. Roger rolled himself up in them and let himself cry until his breathing slowed and steadied and he dropped off to sleep.

The world seemed brighter in the morning. After the initial

shock of waking up and remembering what had happened, Roger flung the curtains open to let in the sunlight. He and Peace had had a stupid argument, that was all. He would make it up to her and everything would go back to normal.

Except he couldn't find her.

She wasn't at the coffee shop, or any of her usual Village hangouts. Frank, when he emerged from his bedroom mid-afternoon, flat out denied all knowledge of her whereabouts before grabbing half a loaf of bread and diving back into his lair. Roger even dared, bristling a little, to enter the murky garage where Weird worked as a motorcycle mechanic. Weird didn't seem to care about anyone, so if he knew where Peace was he'd probably spill. But the coyote shook his head.

"You okay, man?" he asked, something akin to concern in his milky eyes.

"Yeah. Thanks," Roger replied, surprised and a little shamed.

There was nothing for it but to go back to college the next day. Roger was grateful when Brian plopped into his usual seat beside him. Here was one friend he hadn't lost, though he richly deserved to.

"Peace phoned me last night. She told me what happened."

Roger clasped his paws together. Peace had phoned? From where? Had she left a number?

"I'm sorry, Brian. I was out of line," he made himself say.

"I'm sorry I messed things up between you," the puma said, giving Roger's black paw a pat.

"No, no, it was all me. Um, did Peace say where she was?"

Brian shook his head. "I think she might have been at a station—I could hear a train whistle."

At this news, Roger slumped forward in his seat and put his head on his arms. "I was so stupid," he said. "Accusing you and her of—I'm so sorry."

"It's okay, Roger," Brian said. "It's kind of funny, really, because..." He tailed off. When Roger raised his head to look at him, the puma was blushing under his whiskers and Roger realised what Peace had meant by 'apart from anything else'.

"Oh. Ohhh. Oh, Bry, I can't believe how stupid I am." Roger's world had shifted yet again, but Brian was still Brian, his friend, and probably had a tough time ahead of him. He nudged the puma in the ribs to show that he wasn't afraid of him.

Brian gave him a shy, grateful smile. "I hope you find Peace and make it up," Brian said.

"Me too."

"She's really helped me work out who I am."

"Me too, Bry. Me too."

If Peace didn't want to be found right now, Roger had to respect that. Respecting your friends' choices and letting them do their own thing was almost a religion with Frank, and some of that had rubbed off on the raccoon.

He tried hard to pretend that his life could go back to the way it had been before he met her. He resumed his old habits and routines, threw himself into his college assignments, and ignored the constant feeling of emptiness in his stomach. Soon he grew so used to its presence that he was able to accept it, even though it felt as though he was dragging a rock around inside him. Missing Peace? More like missing a piece.

Peace wasn't the only one quitting town, it seemed. One morning, as Roger set off for college, he almost collided with Wade, coming up the steps from the basement with his backpack on his shoulders.

"Oh, hey!" the beaver said. "My ride came through—I'm leaving for Canada. I said goodbye to Frank last night, but you'd gone to bed and I didn't want to bug you. Don't worry, I picked up down there. It's all nice and tidy."

"Glad things are working out for you," Roger said, "and thanks for fixing the ceiling."

"No problem. Thanks for letting me—what was it Frank said?—rack up some Zs."

The nascent lawyer within Roger stirred and perked up its ears. "Zees? Not zeds?"

"Huh?"

"You're not really Canadian, are you, Wade?"

"I never said I was!"

He hadn't. And Frank hadn't. Roger had just assumed, because the guy dressed like a lumberjack and had a maple leaf patch on his knapsack. And if he was headed to Canada, and he wasn't Canadian, and he hadn't wanted anyone to know he was hiding out in Roger's basement...

"Take care, Wade. Send us a postcard."

"I will. Thanks again, and thank Frank for me, too."

Oh, Roger would thank Frank, all right. That evening he lay in wait until the fox sauntered in.

"Wade is a draft dodger."

"Oh, he told you?"

"No, I worked it out." Roger was annoyed both by Frank's lack of an apology and his assumption that Roger would never have found out the truth for himself. "I'm a law student, Frank. Harboring a draft dodger could really mess with my chances."

"And being dead could really mess with Wade's chances. Canada's his best shot, and I hope he makes it. He doesn't have the escape route that we have, because he can't afford college."

"*I'm* studying for a law degree because I want to be a lawyer," Roger said, rather coldly.

"Come on, man. If you hadn't enrolled already, you'd have

signed up pretty quick. I can't see you waving an M60 around—and I mean that in the nicest possible way."

"You know that homosexuals are 4-F, right? Why not just stand up in front of the draft board and tell them you're gay?"

Frank flashed his teeth. "It's no fun telling them something that's true."

"Such a fox he is!"

"Plus, ah, my folks might not go for it."

"Right. Look, Frank...next time just tell me up front, okay? Not that there's going to *be* a next time," Roger added quickly.

"I'm sorry I tricked you. And thanks. You did a good thing, even if you didn't know you were doing it." He began to slink upstairs, but stopped halfway up. "Roger? If it wasn't for the law —would you have been so cut up about Wade trying to skip the draft?"

Roger genuinely didn't know, and he wished, not for the first time, that he'd discussed the war with Peace. It was just one of many topics he'd always avoided, fearing an argument, but she might have helped him get his own views straight.

"I'm glad Wade's going to be okay," he said at last. Frank nodded.

"I couldn't stop the war, but I maybe saved one kid. You, too, whether you knew it or not."

Peace had known Wade's secret, he realised, remembering what she'd said the day Frank was arrested. But she hadn't trusted him with it—or, no, she'd assumed he knew what was going on in his own home. He wished he could tell her that the beaver had gone safely on his way.

"I just miss her so much," he said to Jane. "And I don't know where she is, and I'm worried about her. I don't think she'd do anything stupid—not over me, I'm not worth it—but I made her unhappy and I can't even apologise. That's all I want—to say sorry. After that it'd be okay if I never saw her or spoke to her again. I guess I'd still be sad but at least I wouldn't feel so guilty."

Jane nodded and stroked the back of his wrist. She'd heard all this before, first in choppy sentences punctuated by sobs, then in long, rambling detail on the bleachers while they watched Brian practice, or over colas and a plate of fries in the diner. Every time, she listened and nodded and patted and stroked, murmuring the things Roger wanted to hear: it would be all right, it wasn't his fault, he was okay, it was all okay.

Today, she said, "Roger? I'm sorry, but you need to stop talking about this now."

"Why?"

"Because I think I might be falling for you a bit, and that would be awkward for everyone."

"Would it?" Jane was soft, and she was kind, and she was *here*. It would have been better for Roger if he'd managed to fall in love with someone like this in the first place.

Roger's paw brushed her cheek. She didn't resist as he pulled her in and kissed her mouth, but when his tongue parted her lips to explore her top teeth, she braced her paws against his chest and struggled free.

"*No*, Roger." Her glasses had misted up. "You're still in love with Peace. I'm not being a Band-Aid for your heart and I'm not playing Betty to Peace's Veronica. *And* I don't want to mess up being friends with you because I've got few enough friends as it is, okay?"

"What do you need me to do?" He folded his arms across his chest as if he'd burned them on the chipmunk's fur.

"First, you have to stop telling me all about your broken heart, because it just makes you really adorable. Now forget everything I've said in the last five minutes, and I'll forget you kissed me. Give it a couple days and you're going to regret making that move, mister." Her tone was jokey, but her voice was squeakier than normal. Couple days? Roger regretted it already. He lifted his paws to give her a friendly hug, then let them drop to his sides. He'd forfeited that privilege, for now.

"Are we still friends?" he asked.

"Sure. I've just got a crush on you, that's all. No big deal. It'll wear off." Jane twisted round and made a show of grooming something invisible out of her tail with her claws. Roger cleared his throat.

"Anything I can do to make it wear off quicker? I could be real nasty to you."

Jane snorted.

"You don't believe me? Just watch."

"Don't you dare." She gave him a quick smile and scampered off, her fuzzy tail flicking up and down.

From then on, Jane would only hang out with him if Brian was there. The friendly one-of-the-guys digs in the ribs and pats on the shoulder stopped, and conversation felt awkward. She didn't ask to come back to Roger's place again, and Roger didn't invite her.

"I feel like I'm losing everyone," he said to Frank. The fox was fixing his famous chili, and Roger had come into the kitchen to see what was with all the smoke.

"I thought you liked your space, man."

"What would I do with a spaceman? Take him to my leader?"

"That's not even funny, man."

They both giggled anyway.

"I know what you mean, though," Frank said. "No Peace. No Jane. No Moon. This place is turning into a frat house."

"Where's Moon tonight?"

"Working. That dentist makes her work all the hours she's

got, at no notice, or he'll fire her. And he doesn't believe in massages, or mantras, or all the other stuff she does to calm the patients down. She really needs a new job."

"At least you've got a chance to catch up on your college work," Roger said, raising an eyebrow.

Frank folded his ears back and put his head on one side, eager to please. "Dissertation's almost done, man!"

"Really? Good going! What's it on, again?"

"Ginsberg's *Howl*. Think the profs will go for it?"

"I'm...not sure."

Now Frank had started talking to Roger, he didn't seem able to stop.

"Listen, there's a big music festival out of town next weekend. We're taking Weird's van. You in? The Airplane are headlining."

"The who?"

"Nah, they couldn't make it."

"I think I'll pass. Thanks."

"How come Brian doesn't come around any more? Is he mad at you? Is he mad at *me*?"

"No, no. I think he feels bad about what happened." Roger wasn't too keen on talking about it himself.

"Well, invite him over, man! I'll make chili! In fact,"—Frank spooned a helping into a Tupperware box—"you can bring him a free sample!"

"Okay, okay, okay!"

Roger put Frank's offering in the icebox, once it had cooled. Next morning, he discovered that Frank had eaten it in the night.

He meant to pass on the fox's invitation, he really did, but it slipped his mind. The end of year exams had snuck up on him, and when he wasn't frantically studying, he was sleeping. It helped push thoughts of Peace out of his head, at any rate, or at least keep them at the back of his mind, like a bruise that doesn't hurt if you don't press it. The three of them, Roger, Brian and Jane, studied together, confining their conversation to complaints and commiseration. Sometimes one of them, usually Jane, offered to get coffee or sandwiches. If it was Brian who made the offer, Jane generally went with. Roger wondered if it was all about Jane's unwillingness to be left alone with him, or if it was something more. Should he warn Jane that Brian wouldn't be interested in dating her? He was probably jumping to conclusions again, he decided, and anyway, Jane's love life definitely wasn't his business.

Just once, though, Brian looked up from the textbook he was reading, his nose wrinkled against the dust, and asked "How do you know if someone's interested in you?"

He was staring straight ahead, not looking at either of his friends. Roger rubbed the bridge of his muzzle, and raised an eyebrow at Jane, who shrugged.

"You don't," Roger whispered back. "But if you're interested in someone, you should tell them. It can be embarrassing, but if they're a real friend they won't hold it against you, and it could even lead to something wonderful."

"No talking!" snapped the librarian, rattling her quills. In unison, Roger, Brian and Jane lowered their heads to their notebooks and began scribbling furiously.

Hard Rain

Peace might have ended the Cold War between Roger and his roomie, but without her around, the gap between them widened again and they went back to their old ships-that-pass-in-the-night routine, sliding in and out of kitchen and bathroom and nodding politely when they met on the stairs. Now the exams were over, Brian sometimes dropped by to see Roger. If Roger wasn't there, Frank would let Brian in and make him coffee. Roger imagined Frank was a poor conversational substitute for Peace, but at least Brian had someone who understood him. Probably.

Moon and the others still came round, too, usually while Roger was at college. Since the evening Peace had left, nobody smoked, and the books and beer cans that used to litter the floor were tidied away. Peace never came, though Roger checked the room every night in the hope of finding a lingering trace of linsang scent or a few hairs from that incredible tail.

One evening he noticed as he passed the living-room that the music coming from the record player wasn't as loud as usual, or as...noisy. It was a female voice, with a warbling, trilling quality. He couldn't make out the words, but something about the way the singer sang them reminded him how very lonely he was. He leaned against the wall and listened, with his paws clasped across his stomach.

He'd started accepting Frank and his friends for Peace's sake, but they'd become part of his life too and he missed them. He'd felt as if there was a huge gulf between him and them, but really it was just a closed door.

There were people in there. People who might be strange and annoying but who accepted everyone, maybe even someone who'd goofed the way Roger had.

Roger wanted people.

He opened the door.

"Hey," he said.

"Hey!" Frank replied, sounding pleased. Tom and Anna were lying on the carpet in the kind of fantastic curl only a cat can manage, heads on each other's bellies. They waved. Moon turned from the window, where she had been looking out at the rainy street, and smiled. No sign or smell of Weird. Roger perched himself on one of the beanbags that had materialized in his living-room since Frank's arrival. The filling shifted under him and he sank into its embrace.

"What's the music?" he asked.

"That's Joanie," said Frank reverently.

"Joan Baez," Anna filled in. "The song's called 'Love Is Just A Four-Letter Word'."

"I like her voice. Is she a dog?" Roger leaned cautiously back, rustling as he did.

"Half-coyote," Anna said. "Isn't she trippy?" It was the longest conversation Roger had ever had with her.

They listened companionably—Frank, Moon, Tom, Anna, and Roger—until the song ended. The needle reached the centre of the record and bump-skip-bumped against the hole, making the speakers pop. Frank rose and put another 45 on.

"You'll like this," he promised Roger, passing him the sleeve.

Two voices sang over a guitar, in an echoing harmony that made Roger's tail fluff up and the fur along his shoulders prickle. He turned the sleeve over in his paws, and never once thought of commenting that 'The Sounds of Silence' was an oxymoron.

"That's beautiful," Roger said when it ended. "I thought it was all just noise!"

"*Weird* listens to 'just noise'," Tom put in.

Anna poked him in the ribs. "Meanie."

"And you're still hung up on the Beatles," the black cat continued.

"The Beatles aren't...far out?" Roger asked. His mother didn't approve of the Beatles, so surely Frank and his friends did? They laughed at that, but not in a nasty way, and Frank shuffled through the stack to see if Roger might like the Byrds too.

Roger had never spent an evening quite like this one before. When his mother put on a record, always classical, the rest of the family was expected to sit in attentive, unfidgeting silence until the end, when they would discuss the performers' interpretation of the piece. His father had a few jazz EPs which he played quietly and secretively after everyone else had gone to bed.

Frank played song after song from a stack of 45s. Some Roger liked, some he didn't. The ones he liked, Frank or one of the others told him what it was called and who was singing it. They talked over the music—they talked over the music!—about songs and singers or completely unrelated topics. Frank took out his guitar and played along with some of the songs, or just held the instrument in his lap and stroked it. Moon sat cross-legged on the floor and tapped out a beat on her knees. Anna crooned softly along to her favorites. Frank's rules: do your own thing, have a beautiful scene.

Moon and the cats said goodbye around ten and let

themselves out. Frank sighed and hauled himself out of the couch.

"Coffee?"

Roger accepted the offer of a cup of his own coffee, and Frank padded off to the kitchen, leaving the latest record spinning.

Years down the line, the opening bars would still transport Roger back to that living-room with his mother's carpet and Frank's beanbags, and how it felt to be sitting there late on a rainy evening, with Peace gone, listening to a song that seemed to be all about him and his situation—a song about someone the singer longed to hold in his arms, but who was so elusive, he might as well try and catch the wind.

"Grooving on Donovan there, huh?" The fox studied him from the doorway. "You were really grokking it, weren't you?" he added, putting Roger's mug on the floor beside him. "I've never seen you look that way before."

Roger understood the meaning if not the vocabulary, and nodded, his eyes wet. "I really blew it, didn't I?"

"Yeah, man, you did," Frank said. His ears lowered. "Why'd you have to be such a flake? If I wasn't a committed peacenik I'd have kicked your tail clear to Pittsburgh the night she left!"

Usually Roger would have found the threat as ludicrous as the language in which it was delivered, but this time Frank looked as if he just might mean it. His principles about not interfering with other people's scenes seemed to have fallen by the wayside. Roger shrank back into the beanbag; he was small compared to Frank anyway, and the fact that he was seated made the fox loom over him.

Frank glared down at him. "At least *Davy* was only doing his job."

It was the first time Roger had heard him say that name since the arrest. Frank's jaw clenched and his cheek twitched, then suddenly he was in tears.

Roger knew what he had to do, but it was still difficult. Awkwardly, he stood up, wrapped his short arms around the fox and patted his shoulders. Then he took Frank's paw and pulled him down into the beanbag.

Frank hugged him back.

"I'm sorry I got so angry," he said. "I guess that wasn't just about you and Peace." He clung to Roger, burying his head in the raccoon's shoulder.

"Please tell me where she is, Frank."

"She blew town," Frank said at last. "She's gone to stay with her folks for a while. That's all I know. It...it wasn't all about you, man. This thing's been brewing for a while."

"Okay. Thanks." Frank was right—Peace had been acting weird before she left, and Roger hadn't done anything about it. A candle flame of hope lit in his chest. After all, nobody had actually said they were breaking up. Right?

Frank's breathing was still shuddery. Roger patted his back, then the pats turned to strokes and he felt the fox grow more relaxed. Finally he held Frank the way he'd have held Peace, and gently rocked him. It couldn't fill the linsang-shaped cavity inside him, but it felt somehow right.

When his legs started to go to sleep, Roger rolled Frank off of him. He stayed curled up on the beanbag; his ears flicked at Roger's "Good night," but he didn't move. By the time Roger got up the next morning, he was gone.

It felt as though nothing would ever change, at least until the new semester started. But then Tom and Anna broke up.

"They'll get back together," Frank said. "They always do. And then—*moochas smoochas.*"

"Maybe not this time, Frank," Moon said, serving herbal tea. "I saw Anna at the health food store and she said they were through for good. Her aura was like a brick wall."

Weird just grunted. Roger wondered for the first time if the coyote had a girlfriend, or a boyfriend; if he'd had his heart broken once and locked it away after, or if he simply wasn't interested. He wasn't expecting any answers.

He certainly wasn't expecting Tom to come find him in the kitchen the next evening, his sleek black tail drooping, and start telling Roger all about it.

"We've been together so long, man, it's like part of me is missing."

Roger hadn't been with Peace for as long as all that, but he knew what Tom meant. He nodded.

"I miss her so much."

Nod.

"I'd do anything to get her back."

Nod. It was comforting to know he wasn't alone; Roger sometimes thought that nobody else in the entire history of the world could possibly have felt the way he was feeling. Surely it wasn't common, otherwise how could politicians, surgeons, lawyers and soldiers do their jobs?

"What should I do?"

Roger caught himself in the middle of another nod, realizing that something more was required of him.

"You're asking me? I'm not exactly a shining example of how to get your girl back. I can't even find mine."

"I'm sorry, I just...it's nice to talk to someone who understands."

Yes, it was, but they needed more than that. Roger had to help Tom, he decided. It might be too late for him and Peace, but if he could get one good thing out of this mess, then...that was something. Right? Right.

"How come you split up?" he asked the cat.

"It was stupid," Tom began. Of course it was. "She wanted us to join the Peace Corps after college and I said no way. So she said she'd go on her own and I said that was the dumbest thing I'd ever heard. She called me an oppressive patriarch and left." He shook his head. "I mean. How could Anna cope, out in some jungle? She wouldn't find any vegan chow out there, or...or makeup."

He turned away to get a glass of water, running the faucet too hard so the water sprayed out the sink. Roger scratched his head. It was obvious what Tom had done wrong, but hadn't Roger done exactly the same to Peace? Assuming he knew what was best for her, wanting to look after her because he didn't think she could manage on her own? Implying she maybe wasn't as clever as he was?

"Respect," he said.

"Huh?"

"You didn't respect her as a person. You didn't trust her to make her own decisions and cope on her own, so she's gone off to prove that she can. Why didn't you want to join the Peace Corps?"

"I...guess I was scared. I've never been out of the country... out of the state, even. I'm not very good at all that practical stuff, I'm not good with kids. And there'll be guys out there who are, and I thought maybe Anna would prefer one of them to me. Then I'd be stuck in a jungle on my own."

Jealousy with a side order of paranoia. Roger knew that one too.

"And if you were in the jungle, and there were lots of girls there who looked really hot in the uniform?"

"I'd only have eyes for Anna, I swear."

"So why not give Anna the same credit?"

"...shit." Tom licked the back of his paw and passed it across his ear. "I gotta find her and apologize. Think she'll listen?"

"Just don't try and force her to," Roger advised.

Tom grasped his paw, shook it, and hurried away.

"Hey man, that was a nice thing you did there." Frank slid into the kitchen and began combing the cupboards for snacks. "Ooh! Goldfish crackers!"

"I'm the biggest hypocrite in the world, Frank," Roger said.

"No you're"—Frank swallowed his mouthful of cracker—" not! You passed on what you've learned. You're on a journey, you've made a big step, and you've helped someone else along too."

"Do you think Peace is at the end of my journey?"

"What am I, a guru?" Frank swished his tail. "The destination's not important. It's the traveling. And, yeah, the traveling companions too. They're all part of it, even if they don't go the whole way with you." He looked wistful for a moment, then brightened.

"Hey, that music festival's this weekend," he said. "Simon and Garfunkel will be there! You like them, right?"

Roger had got into some of Frank's music, sure, but a whole weekend of it, not to mention several hours each way crammed in a van filled with hippies and driven by a mad coyote, sounded a bit too much. And where would they sleep?

"I think I'll pass, thanks."

"Okay, but the offer's still open. I'll even stand you a ticket. I guess I've eaten enough of your food to owe you."

Frank made his offer several times over the week that followed, and each time Roger refused. Sometimes he wondered if he was making a mistake, missing out on a good time. He even wondered about meeting a girl there, hooking up, no strings attached. But he knew he'd be thinking about Peace and any such arrangements wouldn't be fair on the girl or on himself.

By the end of the next week he was looking forward to having his house (or Uncle Bob's house, as he still thought of it) to himself for a whole weekend. So it was an unpleasant surprise when he returned home on Friday afternoon to find Frank, Weird, Tom and Anna (now back to holding paws) sprawled on his furniture in attitudes of despair.

"My van's kaput," explained Weird.

"Will you take us in your car?" asked Frank.

"All of you?"

"All of us...and Peace," Frank said. "Please? We'll pay gas, and feed you, and get you into the show."

"Peace is back? Why didn't you tell me?"

Frank's face went extra foxy.

"I thought, if I got the two of you to the festival...I don't know, man."

"Who knew you were such a romantic?" Roger couldn't decide if he wanted to give Frank a hug or punch him. "So that's why you've been bugging me about it."

"I also want you there because you'll enjoy it, and it'll be cool to have you," Frank insisted. The others nodded, and Roger admitted to himself that they didn't look like hippies trying to bum a free ride. They looked like friends.

"Look, Frank, I can't just show up like the prize in the Cracker Jack box," he said. "Peace might not want to hang out with me."

"So what are you going to do about it?" Tom asked quietly. He arched a shoulder, flexed round and licked it.

Roger thought about this for a moment. He walked out of the living-room, closed the door behind him, then picked up the phone in the hallway and dialled the number he'd given up trying weeks ago.

When he returned, a storm of conversation broke out as everyone tried hard to pretend they hadn't been listening in.

"So?" Frank asked. "Do we get a ride?"

"Well...all right. But no smoking in the car."

Frank grinned, and his ears perked up. "Got it," he said.

Road Trip

Roger swung his great-uncle's overloaded Plymouth, camping gear strapped to the roof and hippies hanging out the windows, up the ramp and onto the highway, grateful to be free of the traffic-heavy city.

He'd been afraid that seeing Peace again would be awkward. All she'd said on the phone was that would be fine, thanks for asking. In the event, he'd had to stop the car in a no-parking zone with the engine running, and a cop on the next corner had spotted them. Frank and the others yelled at Peace to hurry up, she threw herself into the back seat across Tom, Anna and Weird, and they drove off with a screech of tires, the linsang's long tail streaming in the wind and everyone giggling madly.

"Whoo! Bet you never burned rubber before!" Weird grinned. Roger had to admit that he hadn't. He laughed along with the coyote, while making a mental note to check the tires were still legal as soon as they stopped for a break.

Frank, who had called shotgun, was fiddling with the radio. The other four, squeezed together in the back, giggled and shoved like kids, keeping an eye out for VW Beetles so they could be the first to shout "Slug Bug!" and punch a fellow-passenger. Any minute, Roger thought, someone would ask if they were there yet or demand to stop and use the restroom.

It would have been an impossible squash if Moon had been there too, but according to Frank she couldn't get the time off work. Roger's suspicion was confirmed: Moon, out of all of Frank's buddies, was the one with the secret core of responsibility and reliability.

Frank's guitar was on the roof rack, out of reach, but Weird produced his harmonica and started a blues tune that made Roger think of lonesome prairies. Maybe this was the coyote's way of howling? It made the fur on Roger's neck and arms prickle, but it wasn't unpleasant. Frank switched the radio off and they all quietened to listen.

"Can we have a bathroom break?"

Roger was all set to be mad at the delay, but it was Peace, and it was the first time she had spoken directly to him since a rushed hello-thanks-for-the-ride as she bounced into the car.

"Sure," he said. He pulled into the next rest stop, which boasted two gas pumps and a hamburger stand. Frank made a beeline for the food, while the others queued to take possession of the bathroom key. Peace emerged first, shaking her wet paws, and crossed to Roger, who had seated himself on a patch of grass in the shade of the Plymouth.

"Hey," Roger said.

"Hey."

All sorts of questions and requests shot through Roger's mind, but what came out was "Here, use my sweater."

"Thanks." She tugged the front of his overshirt around her damp paws, her knuckles brushing the fur of Roger's stomach. He shivered a little. She was so close, so intimate—but that was Peace, always at ease with her body and other people's. It didn't mean they were back together, but maybe it meant they were friends?

"Peace?" he said. The small paws disentangled themselves from his clothes. Roger made no move to keep them there, although part of him wished linsangs took longer to dry. "You might not want to talk about what happened, and I guess you don't want us to go back to the way we were, but I can't not say how sorry I am."

Peace sat beside him, wrapping her arms around her knees. Frank shot them a sharp glance and steered the other three away around the corner of the gas station.

"And I'm sorry I ran away," she said. "It was just all too much. I went back to my parents to sort out where my head was at."

"So...where is your head at?"

"Not the same place as my parents' heads, that's for sure!" She gave a sharp-toothed smile Roger couldn't help returning. "They kept on at me to go back to college, and I remembered how mad I got when you said the same thing. Then I got to thinking that maybe people say that stuff because they care about you. And that not everything your folks think is automatically wrong."

Roger rubbed her between the shoulders, because it seemed like the right thing to do.

"I don't know about us yet, Roger. I like you very much—and that means you can hurt me very much too, and I can hurt you. Let's just be friends, for now, and have a good time this weekend, okay? Can we do that?"

"Sure," Roger said automatically. Friends was better than nothing, and she hadn't ruled out getting back together, had she? He resolved to be on his very best behavior all weekend and win Peace back.

He blew it in half an hour.

Peace called shotgun after their rest stop. Frank opened his mouth to argue that his claim was valid for the entire journey, caught Roger's eye, and held the door open, bowing low.

Rain spattered on the windshield, and Roger set the wipers going. Their slow arcs and the soft whine of rubber on glass was hypnotic, the drumming of water on the roof and the swish of the tires soothing. The cats were asleep in each other's arms within a mile, Frank following suit, while Weird stared out the window, humming to himself. They left the highway for a narrower country road.

"I love the rain," Peace said.

"Yeah? Maybe when I'm safe at home with a cup of cocoa. Not when I'm driving. Or when I'm about to spend a weekend in a tent, in a field."

"It's just part of nature, Roger. You shouldn't try to hide from nature."

Maybe it was the car that cut in front of them, making Roger work hard with the brakes and steering-wheel to avoid a collision on the wet tarmac, that made him snap. After all, Peace's beloved nature had just tried to kill him.

"That's dumb," he said.

Peace gave a little squeak and shrank back in her seat as if he'd slapped her. Roger clenched his teeth. He'd done it again— hurt her, and so easily. Criticised her beliefs and made out she was stupid. Got close, then pushed away. Forwards, backwards, backwards, forwards. On and on. Was that how it was always going to be? No way could he deal with a whole weekend of it, completely out of his element, wet and uncomfortable, and fighting pointlessly with the love of his life.

"I can't do this," he said, pulling on to the shoulder. He turned off the ignition, tossed the keys to Frank blinking and stretching in the back seat. Even as they landed in the fox's paw, he knew he should have given them to Peace, that it looked as if he didn't trust her or didn't think women could drive, but what difference would it make? It was only the last in a long series of mistakes. A relationship-ful.

"Enjoy the festival." He looked for traffic, opened the door and stepped out into the light rain. Three, four steps down the road, then he jogged back to the car.

"Er...you do have a license, right?"

Frank, stunned, just nodded, cradling the keys in his palms.

Roger walked away again and, this time, resolutely did not turn around. He heard a door slam, then another, and the familiar grumble of the Plymouth starting up. Didn't turn around. Heard light, pattering footsteps hurry after him. Didn't turn around. Felt fingers slip into his, smelled jasmine, and stopped, joyfully...only to see that his paw was being held not by Peace, but by Anna.

"The others thought we should leave you to cool off," she said, "but I couldn't let you just walk away like that."

"Well. Thanks, I guess," Roger said, managing a small smile. They walked in silence for a while, Roger grateful to have someone close by even if it wasn't the someone he wanted.

"So, you and Tom..." he said at last.

"Yeah." Anna was obviously trying not to look too happy, in deference to Roger's situation, but her eyes were shining. "And we're applying to the Peace Corps next summer! Did he tell you what he did?"

Roger shook his head.

"Stood under my window singing 'In My Life'. I asked him what he'd have done if I hadn't let him in, and he said he'd have gone through the Beatles' entire back catalogue."

"That's cute."

"Maybe you could do something like that for Peace?"

"I don't know about that. I can't sing."

"You don't have to sing. Just show her that you care, and you value her, and you listen to her. You're the first guy she's gone with, Roger. I know she seems super-confident all the time, but she's nervous just like you."

"The first?" Roger had always assumed...well, that Peace was the kind of girl his mother had warned him about. He'd never asked because he didn't want to know. "But she's on the Pill," he said.

"Listen. Just because you can do something, doesn't mean you gotta. And just because you don't want to do something, doesn't mean you shouldn't fight for your right to do it."

Roger digested this, trite hippie nonsense though it sounded. Nothing was ever as simple as Anna, or Frank, made out. Nothing.

"But that song," he said, remembering their first date. "'Song for Joe'. I can't imagine writing something like that if you'd never gone with anyone. I've been jealous of Joe ever since I first heard it. Don't tell me there is no Joe!" He tried to laugh, but it came out more like a sob.

"There's a Joe." Anna stopped walking but didn't let go of Roger's paw, so he was tugged back. He looked into her eyes, puzzled.

"Joe was Peace's kid brother," she said. "He died when he was three."

Roger searched for the words to express his horror and shock, but he couldn't find them. "I didn't know," he said.

"She doesn't talk about it. I asked her about the song, once—like you, I thought he was some guy who broke her heart. And I guess, in a way, he was."

"Poor Peace." Why hadn't she told him? He'd have...well, he'd have held her, and kissed her, and told her how sorry he was, and it wouldn't have been anything like adequate, but he would have been doing his best.

"You two are very alike, you know," Anna said. Roger tilted

his head. He'd thought they were total opposites—that was the source of both their attraction and their problems.

"You both shut down about the things that hurt you. You both run away when stuff gets heavy," the cat continued. "Peace ran from you and now you're running from her. You guys should try just talking it out."

Roger remembered how he had felt when Peace ran out his front door. Had she felt the same when he exited the car? For a moment, he hoped so—then he remembered that he'd do anything rather than hurt Peace.

"I think I want to go back to the others," he said. He'd heard the car drive off, but maybe they could hitch a ride?

"Turn around," Anna told him.

On the opposite side of the road, the Plymouth was bumping along at a discreet distance, the engine just biting. Frank had only pulled away to turn it around. Anna gave a thumbs up, and the fox hit the gas, turned again, and pulled up next to them.

"I'm sorry, guys," Roger said as Frank switched seats again.

"It's cool. Sometimes we all need space." Weird, the speaker, was jammed into the corner of the car by Tom's knees. He grinned as he realized the incongruity, and the other passengers laughed harder than the joke deserved.

Peace leaned over to change the radio station. "Thanks for coming back," she whispered, her head close to Roger's.

"I won't run away again," he promised her, flicking water from his ears. Peace snaked her tail down to brush against his cold ankles.

"Me either," she said.

"Right, this should be our turnoff. Turnoff to turn on, heh... whoa." Frank, map-reading, looked up and saw what Roger had already noticed: a queue of slow-moving traffic clogging the side road.

"Heavy," complained Weird. He curled up in his corner of the car and fell instantly asleep.

"Is this all for the music festival?" Roger asked, more than an hour later. They made barely any progress for the first twenty minutes, less for the next twenty. After that, they didn't move at all. The rain got heavier.

"I guess," Peace said, disappointment in her voice. "I really wanted to see the opening group."

"We'll be lucky to catch the closing group," grumbled Tom, craning out the window. More cars had joined the queue behind them; they were committed to their route, else Roger would have turned round and headed for home some time ago.

"Hey! Look what those guys are doing!" Roger looked in the direction Tom was pointing. Two gibbons, whooping and shrieking, were running along the line of cars, jumping from roof to roof. The cars they landed on bounced and shook, but the occupants didn't seem to mind. Roger braced himself as footsteps crossed his own roof, and his passengers cheered.

Other attendees were walking alongside the stuck cars, like pilgrims or refugees, carrying tents and bags. Peace turned to Roger, and he knew immediately what she was going to ask.

"Can we?"

"There's still a mile to go, Peace. But if you can manage it, you guys go ahead. I'll park the car."

"Everyone's just abandoning their cars, man. You'll be here all night," Frank said.

"It doesn't feel right to leave it on the public highway like this. What if there was an emergency? No—go on. I'm not as into this scene as you, anyway."

Frank grinned and rubbed his nose, aware he was being

mocked. Peace put her paw on Roger's and unhooked the black fingers one by one from the wheel.

"But I want to go with *you*," she said.

That did it.

"Everybody out," Roger said. His backseat passengers emerged and stretched gratefully before grabbing their luggage. Roger applied the handbrake, rolled up the windows and locked the doors before following. The car in front had already been abandoned, which eased his conscience a little.

Roger tried not to stare at their fellow travelers, but it was hard. Some had beads and braids in their fur, some were topless, all wore a bizarre mixture of clothes that looked as though they'd been picked out of a dumpster behind the Salvation Army. He soon decided it was safer, and more pleasant, to look at Peace, who at least returned his stares with smiles. They didn't talk much, but Peace held Roger's paw and Roger gripped hers back.

'Just friends' didn't hold paws. Did they? Did they if they were Peace?

Roger didn't want to spoil the magic by asking if they were back together. He was sure he'd know if they were. Wouldn't he?

At last they stepped over a ridge to see a patchwork city of tents and camper vans spread out below them. Fires had been lit against the gathering dusk, and bodies in sleeping-bags—sometimes two or more to a bag—sat around the campsite despite the rain, faces and ears turned to the stage in the distance. Waiting.

"Ooh—samosas!" said Frank, and headed for a food stall from which strange, spicy smells were wafting. Weird, paws on hips, looked from Tom and Anna to Roger and Peace.

"You guys go watch the show," he said. "I'll pitch the tent."

"You sure?" Roger asked, more as a formality than because he thought he'd be any great shakes at tent-pitching. Anna and Tom had already split, paw in paw.

"Sure. You kids have fun."

Roger squeezed Peace's paw and smiled at her. Then he heard a voice at his shoulder—a familiar voice, polite and soft, but so out of context here it took him a moment to recognize it.

"Hey," Brian said again. "Is Frank with you?"

Roger looked the puma up and down. Brian was wearing an old shirt he sometimes put on at weekends, but now it was unbuttoned, revealing several strings of beads against the creamy fur of his chest. An embroidered headband encircled his ears, with three feathers jammed into the side in Day-Glo shades of green, pink and orange. He looked as comfortable, and as much like he belonged, as he did in the library.

Roger had questions, but the one he asked was "Did you come all the way out here, to the middle of nowhere, to try and find Frank in a crowd of thousands?"

Brian grinned. "It worked, didn't it? Hey, you don't mind, do you? Me muscling in on your scene?"

"This is not my scene!" It wasn't. Was it? "I guess it's everybody's. Good to see you, man."

Frank appeared, his paws full of steaming triangular pastries. He thrust two at Roger and Peace. "Brian! Man!" he spluttered, his mouth full.

"Come on," Peace said. "Let's leave them to it."

They picked their way through the groups and pairs to where the crowd was thicker.

"Closer?" Roger asked, already knowing the answer.

"Closer," grinned Peace.

At last the crowd was too thick to squeeze past, except where a wide patch of mud barred their way.

"I guess this'll do," said the linsang.

"No it won't," Roger said. "Not for you. You gotta be right at the front, right?"

Before Peace could reply, he had lifted her in his arms. She squeaked and wrapped her paws and tail around his neck, tucking her feet up. Roger waded into the mud, ankle-deep, and made his determined way towards the stage. He slipped a couple times, but held on to Peace with an iron grip and recovered himself. Peace clung and giggled, and Roger found himself laughing too, splashing and kicking like a kid in a puddle. Heads began to turn and watch his progress.

"This love thing is hard work," he muttered into Peace's neck, "but...it's worth it." Peace squeezed him tighter.

They arrived on the far side of the slick with a clear path to the stage and Roger set his burden gently down. Not a drop of mud had sullied the linsang's spotted coat or her luxurious tail.

Peace shook her head. "Look at you," she said.

"I'm a mess, huh?" Roger shook his feet one after the other, splaying the toes. He guessed he'd have to wait until he was home to clean under his claws properly.

"No, you're...oh, Roger." She cocked her head. "When you carried me through the mud, you didn't care what you looked like or who was watching. You were in the moment, weren't you? You loosened up at last!"

"Yeah. I suppose I did." Now that she'd mentioned it, of course, he was instantly embarrassed.

"Look around you," she whispered. Roger, cringing, turned around. Everyone there was as ragged and muddy as he was. Nobody thought he'd made a spectacle of himself. In fact, even as he watched, a big dog in a leather jacket put his paws together and clapped. A couple of girls joined in, then their boyfriends, then a whole crowd more. Roger found to his surprise that he was the center of attention—and loving it.

"Here." Peace took the silver peace symbol from around her neck and worked the chain over Roger's head. He touched it with a pad, then dug in his pocket and brought out the bracelet of rainbow stars. He had waited a long time to slip it on to Peace's slim wrist.

His audience clapped harder as Peace held her arm aloft, showing off the sparkles, then flung both paws around Roger and nuzzled into his chest. Bright lights suddenly bloomed, the first notes of an electric guitar sounded, and the applause spread through the whole crowd like lightning and roared like thunder.

The opening act was on.

Peace Out

"That's the last!" Roger put the crate of books on the floor of Frank's old room. "Welcome home, Peace."

The linsang, who was tucking a sheet on to the bed, straightened up and kissed Roger on the nose. Her Indian scarves were already hanging from the walls, and on the bedside table there was a framed picture Roger hadn't seen before, of a laughing baby linsang boy.

"Thanks again, Roger. It'll make a big difference being this close to campus when term starts—not to mention...other amenities." Her paw slipped under Roger's shirt and scritched just above his hip.

"We better start getting ready for the party," Roger said reluctantly.

"I thought Frank and Brian were on it."

"Last I saw they were smooching in the kitchen. I think we need to go keep an eye on them."

"Sure. But I want to thank you properly first."

Roger was expecting another kiss. Instead, Peace seated

herself cross-legged on the crate he'd brought in and reached for her guitar.

"I wrote you a song," she said, suddenly shy. She dropped her gaze to the frets, staring down at them rather than looking at Roger, with a tremble in her voice that wasn't there when she played to dozens at the coffee shop. Roger recognised the tune from when they'd started going out, but it had had no words then.

"So take my hand and come with me
The world is yours and mine
Rainbow stars are shining on you
Let them shine!"

The rainbow stars Roger had given her glittered on her wrist as she strummed. It was more upbeat than anything he'd heard her play before, and he was tapping his foot and smiling by the end of the chorus.

As the last notes died away, Roger opened his eyes.

"Nobody's ever written a song for me before," he said. "I don't think anyone ever will again." He took the guitar from her paws and rested it carefully against the wardrobe before scooping Peace up in his arms and laying her down on the bed. Her tail draped over the foot, twitching.

They might still screw this up between them. They probably would. What were the chances of staying with your first girlfriend for the rest of your lives, and making it work, and staying happy? Pretty low, Roger guessed, but maybe it could happen. And whatever the future held, right now there was a beautiful linsang in his guest room. He hoped she would be sharing his room, too, but he wanted her to have this private space of her own. He lay down beside her on the narrow single bed and put his paw around her shoulders. Not doing. Just being.

A noise from downstairs made his ears flick; a tiny pop that he couldn't immediately identify. It was followed by another, then more, then a rapid hail of them like machine gun fire. They heard Frank's voice say "Whoa!" and a shriek of laughter from Brian.

Roger sat up.

"Are we having popcorn at this party?" Peace asked him.

"We *were*." He sighed. "Let's go see."

The kitchen looked as if an out of season snowstorm had blown through. Under Roger's supervision, Brian and Frank cleaned up the mess they'd made and put out bowls of snacks and punch.

"How's the new digs, doll?"

"Fine, Frank. How are yours?"

"Groovy. Closer to the amenities." The fox grinned at Brian.

"Dare I ask what you're wearing?" Roger asked, eyeing Frank's vibrant orange and yellow shirt. Complicated stitching framed its V neck.

"It's called a *dashiki*," Frank said proudly. "That reminds me —got something for you." He reached in his pocket and pulled out...something. A piece of material decorated with multicolored swirls, in a style Roger believed was called 'psychedelic.' The raccoon turned it over in his paws, wondering.

"It's a tie!" he said at last.

"Yeah! I figured, I'm never going to cure you of wearing them, but you can at least wear a groovy one."

"Thanks." Chuckling, Roger untied the plain red tie from his collar and replaced it with the rainbow.

"It's an electric Kool-Aid acid tie!"

"Brian, I don't even want to know what that means."

"Thanks for hosting this party," Frank added.

"Well, there's a lot to celebrate. Peace moving in, Tom and Anna's engagement...Weird's new van..."

"Frank's new man," Peace put in, smiling at Brian.

Frank put his arm around the puma's shoulders.

"Speaking of the Weirdmobile, you guys are coming on our trip next summer, right? Overland to India?"

Roger mirrored Frank's stance, draping his own arm across Peace's bare back.

"Thinking about it," he said, truthfully but noncommittally. "You haven't invited too many people tonight, have you?"

"No, man, and nobody real crazy, I promise. It's going to be a nice party. And you're bringing some of your less square college friends?"

"Yup. It's time they knew about my secret double life!" Roger flexed his skinny arm in a Superman pose. He might still be nervous about his worlds colliding, but he wasn't going to show it. Not to Frank and not to his fellow students. Especially not to Peace, the one who knew how hard it was for him.

"Their minds are going to be blown, man, blown." Frank put his paw around Brian's waist.

"They sure are." Brian smiled goofily at the fox. "We'll be discreet while the guys are here, though," he added more seriously.

"Oh—mailman came." Frank picked a package off the counter and shook it. "It's addressed to both of us, so I waited for you."

Who would write him and Frank together? Roger checked the stamps: Canadian.

Peace and Brian peered over their shoulders as Frank opened the box. A postcard of Toronto, a bottle of maple syrup, a red and white knit cap, and a sealed can.

"What's that? Cookies?"

Frank opened the lid a crack and took a sniff.

"I think this is for me," he said hastily, tucking it away in a drawer.

"'Dear Guys,'" Roger read. "'I am settled in Toronto with a

good job and a girlfriend. Hope the ceiling is holding up okay. Love, Wade. PS: the hat is called a TUQUE. I'm sure learning my Zeds and Zees now!'"

"That's cute." Peace grabbed the cap and pulled it down over Roger's ears. "And so are you!"

Roger took it off again and ran a paw through his hair. "Anything else I should know before we get the party started?"

"Oh yeah—your mom called," Frank said brightly. "She and your dad are in town and they need somewhere to crash. They'll be here in twenty."

Roger's jaw dropped.

"Kidding!" Frank grinned and held up his paw. Brian slapped his own against it.

"Excuse me while I kiss this guy," he said, giving Frank a peck on the cheek.

An hour later, the party was in full swing. Weird was in charge of the sounds, swapping discs on Uncle Bob's old record player. Roger noticed that Jane was spending a lot of time over there, drinking beers with the coyote and arguing over the music he picked. Good!

Moon had a little group around her. They were holding paws in a circle and chanting something. As Roger watched, the jackrabbit wrinkled her nose at him and winked.

"Hey, Roger!" she called. "Did you hear? I got a new job!"

"Well, that's another reason to celebrate." Roger sat himself down, cross-legged. Peace, walking past, stopped to pet his ears and listen. "What is it?"

"I'm helping usher in the Age of Aquarius," Moon told him.

"Could you be a bit more specific? My careers counselor's never mentioned that as an option."

"She's going to teach kindergarten!" Peace burst out. "Isn't it wonderful?"

"Children are our future," Moon said dreamily, "and I'll be

surrounding them with peace, beauty and harmony right at the start of their trip."

Roger nodded. It was perfect. If he ever had kids of his own (and, with a shy glance at Peace, he filed that thought away for now) he couldn't imagine a better person than Moon to guide them through their early years.

"Congratulations, Moon," he said. "Teach your children well."

Moon beamed.

Frank and Brian had kept their promise, just about. They weren't exactly doing a Tom and Anna—the two cats were dancing, very close—but the fox and the puma were sharing a beanbag and if you were tuned in to such things, you'd have taken them for a couple straight away. Someone to whom the idea of two guys together was alien probably wouldn't notice anything. Satisfied with the way the party was going, Roger trotted into the kitchen to top up the snacks.

He was reaching for the big bag of potato chips he'd hidden at the back of the cupboard, out of sight of Frank, when he felt paws on his waist. He rocked back from his tiptoes into Peace's arms.

"Do you want to go upstairs?" she whispered, nuzzling his neck.

"Now?" Roger had no doubt what she meant; he was just a little worried that the house might burn down without his supervision. He reached back, put his paws on Peace's thighs and pulled her on to him.

"Why not?" she breathed into his ear. "Everyone's doing their thing. Frank and Moon won't let anything bad happen. The place is full of good vibes."

She was right; Roger could feel them. Here, in this house of happiness, and now. It was time. This was what he wanted, and

Peace was the one he wanted it with. Her arms curled round him, and he took hold of her paws.

"Hey." Frank appeared beside them. "Mama Creek wants to rap with you. Great party, man."

Roger and Peace sprang apart, and an elderly otter entered. After a moment's thought, Roger recognised her as his eccentric neighbor, and the gray fox holding her arm looked kind of familiar too. They were an odd couple: the fox in a smart suit, the otter wearing a purple skirt sewn with hundreds of tiny mirrors, her snow-white hair hanging loose down her back. Had they come to complain about the noise?

"Hello, dear. I'm Betty Creek." She smiled, wrinkling her nose. "I know what you're thinking—I'm a little old for this scene. But I prefer to think I was just born a while too soon."

She stood beside him, leaning against the counter, and took a sip from her wineglass. "It's been a while since I saw the inside of this place."

Roger thought about this for a moment. "You knew Uncle Bob?"

"Robert was a dear friend of mine. In his own way, he was quite the hepcat."

"He was?" Roger remembered the family visits, and how they'd stopped with no explanation. He wondered what in particular about being a hepcat had upset his parents.

"He wasn't the marrying kind, as we used to say—much like your charming young friend Frank. This house was a safe place for kids like Frank to hang out or stay for a while. Often they'd been thrown out by their own families, and Bob was like a father to them. And to Spencer—Mr Brennan—here...but I'll let him explain."

Brennan! Roger flashed back to the property developer's office, and his strange behaviour. This, as Frank would say, was getting freaky.

"Robert and I were very close for a number of years," the fox said.

"You weren't at the funeral," Roger said without thinking.

"No. I didn't think that would be wise."

"I'm sorry," said Roger, and meant it. He held out his paw, and the gray fox shook it gravely. All the secrets Roger had tried to hide, he realized, were small ones next to Brennan's and his great-uncle's.

Brennan twinkled at Peace. "This must be the famous girlfriend, the one who works at the coffee shop? Are you going to sing for us later?"

"Uh, maybe?" Peace slipped her paw into Roger's, and he squeezed it. Yes, the evening had turned weird, but in a good way. Music and laughter filled the house where, a few months ago, he had confined his activities to sleeping, studying and getting riled with Frank. He had never felt so surrounded by friends, or so at home.

"I'm so glad Robert left his house to the right great-nephew," said the otter.

"I'm glad too, ma'am," Roger replied. "Now, if you'll excuse me—I have to go get my freak on." He scooped Peace up into his arms and made for the stairs.

"Far out," said Frank.

YOU'VE COME TO THE END, MAN. THIS IS ALL THERE IS.

About the Author

Huskyteer's short stories have been published both in and out of the fandom, and have won two Cóyotl Awards, two Ursa Major Awards, and one Leo Award. She rides a motorcycle, has a black belt in karate, and is much less cool than that makes her sound. Find her at huskyteer.co.uk.

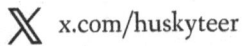 x.com/huskyteer

About the Publisher

FurPlanet Productions is a small press publisher serving the niche market that is furry fiction. They sell furry-themed books and comics published by themselves and most major publishers in the community. If you can't get to a furry convention where they are selling in the dealers room, visit their online stores: FurPlanet.com for print books and BadDogBooks.com for eBooks.

facebook.com/furplanet

x.com/furplanet

animal.business/@furplanet